The
Lives and Deaths
of
Harry Blunt

by Tina Konstant

2nd Edition

Previously published under pen name
Obediah Keane

PEAGLE
PRODUCTIONS

To my remarkable,
wild, beautiful family!

THE DEATH OF HARRY BLUNT

"You have 58 seconds, Mr. Blunt. We have a schedule to keep."

Harry Blunt blinked up at the tall, tall man standing in his bedroom. "You shouldn't be here."

"Yet..." The man took a breath and let it go like he knew he'd be able to catch it later. "Here I am."

Harry was sure he should be alarmed or at least a little offended by the intrusion. It was the canary yellow suit, he decided. Or maybe the ebony bald of the man's head. Harry had never seen a head so polished that the white hanky used to dab it shimmered. But no. It wasn't the suit, or the head, or the hanky, or the tan brogue shoes, or even the smell of lavender that filled the air. It was a thin piece of black thread that dangled from the last letter of an embroidered instruction on the man's jacket pocket: *Call me Grimmer.*

"I'd rather you come back next week. I'll be ready then." The nausea Harry had tolerated every day for the last two years was gone, but that didn't stop the roiling in his gut. He turned on *Call Me Grimmer.* "You can't just spring this kind of thing on a person!"

Grimmer let a smile play on his lips. "Clock's ticking."

Harry pressed his bare feet into the carpet surrounding his bed, pulled his dressing gown tight around him, and stood as tall as his 5'6" frame allowed. "I don't give a flying duck about your clock. I've got goodbyes to say."

Grimmer sighed. "Mr. Blunt, what are you looking for? Leave your toothbrush. You won't need it where you're going."

"What do you mean, where I'm going? I lived a good life. I did good things." Harry pointed to the growing crowd around his cancer-beaten body. "Look at these people. That's Max. We grew up together. He's my oldest and best friend. And Janice and Jake. My neighbours for 20 years. And…" Harry dropped to his hands and knees to look under his bed.

"There's nothing under your bed that you can take with you, and conversation won't delay things. It's time to go. Now."

Harry stood up and swooped his arm around the room slowly filling with people. "Friends, colleagues, neighbours. All coming to mourn me. That wouldn't happen if I hadn't done at least some good."

"The worst people in history are famous for having the biggest funerals, Mr. Blunt. Humans are odd that way." Grim tapped a gold pocket watch with an elaborate engraving of the Tree of Life on the lid. He pointed out the second hand to Harry.

Harry shook his head. "I'm not ready."

"You say that now because you can't see the big picture, but you're perfectly ready. Now is the time."

Three young people walked into the bedroom clinging to each other. Harry forgot his search and ran to them. He was a hand-stretch away. Less. If he curled his fingertips, he'd touch them.

"One last touch, please." He pushed forward but a blast of hot wind shoved him back like he was trying to reach beyond the eye of his own personal hurricane. "These are my kids. They're good kids."

Grim sighed. "I'm sure they are. You can't take them either."

Harry got to his feet and stamped the floor but felt nothing except warm, soft air. "I don't understand how this works."

Grim closed his eyes. For just one instant, Harry wondered how many times the infamous Reaper had heard those words. An instant later, Harry decided he didn't care.

"I raised those kids. Pretty much on my own." Harry pointed out the tall man with dark, serious eyes holding his siblings' hands. "Benjamin Blunt." Harry wrapped his arms around himself, pulling every memory of his son into his heart and feeling it warm. "I named him. He's taking over my company, you know."

"Coat hangers." Grim flipped through his notebook then snapped it shut.

"What? Yes. Coat hangers. Something people will always need. Useful, you see? That was my mission. To create something useful. It was a toss-up between paperclips and coat hangers."

"Mr. Blunt, we absolutely, without question, need to go. Now. Being late isn't an option. Please, don't try to touch them. It's not possible."

"This is Zach."

Grim put his watch back into his pocket. "I know Zach. Artist. Very clever. Let's go."

"But I need you to understand something. See Rainey? My baby girl? Do you actually see her?"

"Sadly, I do, Harry. Seven seconds. Make the most of it. Leave the cash. You can't… Harry. Credit cards aren't accepted."

"I'm a rich man!"

"Good for you. No suitcases allowed."

Harry looked over Grim's shoulder and wondered why the bus pulling up outside his bedroom door belching smoke hadn't surprised him. "You know, I've never enjoyed travelling by bus."

"Four."

"Four seconds? The doctor said I had 18 months!"

"He was being polite."

"I'm only 61 years old."

"Congratulations."

"Can I at least take my slippers?"

Grim sighed. "They're beside the dresser. On either side of that bedpan over there. Are you ready now?"

Harry shook his head. "No. I'm not ready. I can't find the damn things!"

His last words which those gathered around his bed will repeat and repeat were: "If I'm going to meet my maker, I need my non-slip slippers."

▼

Harry Blunt wasn't going to meet his maker. He was taking Seat #87 on Reaper's bus, which had already stopped at London, Seattle, Oslo, Key West, Cape Town, and 19 other destinations. Fairfig, Harry's hometown, almost halfway between the north of Scotland and the south of England, was the last on the route before terminating at Port Harker.

The last thing Harry saw before Grim hissed the doors closed on a luxury tour bus that would look perfectly acceptable on any street in any town anywhere in the world were his three, grownup children clinging to each other with tear-streaked faces.

Ben, tall and strong, already solving problems and keeping things organised and neat. Zach, feeling every inch of his loss, knowing an artist had to feel pain more than anyone else. And Rainey, clinging onto her oldest brother like he was her last precious lifeline in a sea already heaving in time with a rising chaos.

"I did good, didn't I? I did a good job." Harry pressed his hand against the dark, tinted bus window and watched the doctor take charge of his body, a neighbour take charge of a pair of antique, gold cufflinks, and his oldest boy take charge of the family.

"No, Harry," Grim said from the driver's seat. "I can't say you did."

The bus rocked and rumbled, jerked, and heaved like its wheels had been caught in mud and needed a moment to get traction. Someone behind Harry started to sob. Harry ignored it, stood up out of the soft, velvet seat Grim had put him in, then promptly sat when the bus swerved. "What do you mean *I can't say you did*?"

THE TRIP TO PORT HARKER

Pointing to a "Don't Disturb The Driver" sign above his head and swerving the bus far more than Harry thought was necessary, Grimmer leaned forward, flipped open a glove box, and pulled out a stack of envelopes that in size, shape, and colour resembled ones used by every taxman around the world. He waved them above his head. "Marge, will you do the honours?"

A woman who, to Harry, looked 103 but moved like a teenager, leapt out of the seat across the aisle and strode to the front of the bus. "Always a pleasure, Grim." Dressed in blue dungarees over a purple T-shirt and thick socks under firm hiking boots, she looked like she'd been preparing for this trip for a decade at least.

With all the passenger windows blacked out, Harry looked over Grim's shoulder. A boy around eight years old, wearing Ghostbusters swimming trunks, climbed onto the seat next to Harry. He followed Harry's gaze.

"I don't see anything. Do you?"

Harry shook his head. "Just blinking lights."

"Like a runway?"

Harry dug his back into the seat, tightened the belt around his paisley dressing gown, and pressed his feet into his slippers. A girl in the seat in front glanced back and stared at Harry and the boy then turned to face Marge, who flipped through the envelopes, and raised her arms high in the air like a storyteller about to embark on a wild tale of midnight murder, mystery, and mayhem.

"Do it without the fanfare, Marge!" Grim called then turned the wheel left, then right, then left again. The pale lights on the screen in front of him blinked shades of red, yellow, and green. "Like I showed you."

"Bloody hell. Fine." Marge put a smile on her wrinkled face and revealed toothless gums.

The boy stood on his seat to be seen. "There's been a mistake. I shouldn't be here. It's my birthday."

Marge patted him on the shoulder and pushed him back down. "Grim never makes mistakes."

Before Harry had time to suggest that that seemed unlikely in the greater scheme of things, Marge waved the envelopes in the air.

"Right."

A murmur rippled through the bus. Harry turned and looked over his headrest. From the outside, the bus had looked like any bus he'd ever seen. It certainly hadn't looked big enough to fit what he estimated were well over 180 people.

"These envelopes contain your legal papers." Marge's voice bounced all the way to the back of the bus.

People looked at each other. The murmurs gathered.

"You all have tickets across the river."

A skinny man in a three-piece suit waved his hand. "What river? You talking *the* river? We go Hell? You say we go Hell? Is Diablo waiting? Why?"

The murmurs escalated to mutters. Marge held her hands up. "No one's going to Hell."

"Don't make promises, Marge." Grim tapped the steering wheel to a tune Harry couldn't hear. "Just hand the envelopes out. We're running late, thanks to Mr. Blunt."

187 people glared at Harry. He sank low in his seat.

Marge held up the first envelope. "Raise your hand when I call your name. Precious Bundles?"

A young African woman stood, adjusted a large, fluffy, pink bath towel around her, took a step forward, glanced at Harry, then pulled her shoulders back, took her envelope, and sat back down.

"Billamy Bragstone?"

The boy in his swimsuit stood. "Me! Call me Bill. That's me!"

"Good lad. Now, sit back down. Suzie McAuble? No, there's no baggage in the hold. You can only take what you carry. Yes, you have to take your envelope. Alicia Sascoona?"

No one moved. No one raised their hand. "Alicia Sascoona?"

Someone at the back of the bus called out. "I think this might be her. She might have fainted."

"Pass the envelope back. Hector D. Beziuz?"

The skinny man in the three-piece suit stepped into the aisle. "I no gonna go. I no getting off tis bus. I be in control of mine destiny!"

"One out of three isn't bad, Mr. Bezuiz. You are definitely in charge of your destiny. Now, take your envelope, and stop being an idiot."

Hector D. Bezuiz blinked. "Okay. I get off tis bus. But I go cross no river of no kind."

"I don't care what you do when you get there. Just take your damn envelope."

Name after name, Marge handed the envelopes out until she came to the last one. "Harry Blunt?"

Harry stared up at the old woman. "Keep it together, Harry. I don't know what's in here, but you'll work it out. You always do."

Harry studied Marge. No, he'd never met her. He was sure he hadn't. "How do you know? And what makes you think I've got things to work out?"

Marge pointed at the ceiling and smiled. "Just like I know *this* is going to happen…wait for it…" Her smile turned into a grin. "Three. Two. One."

Like Grim and Marge had done this a hundred times, a ping-pong ring that sounded suspiciously like the one in every airport in the world chimed from the roof.

Grim cleared his throat. "It's your driver speaking. Thank you for choosing Port Harker Express. I hope you enjoyed your journey. We'll be arriving at your destination in five…no." The bus tilted to the left, causing people to gasp, scream, and in Alicia Sascoona's case, pass out again. "We've arrived at our destination… Oops." Grim coughed and the bus jerked to what Harry assumed was a standstill. "Sorry about that. New tyres. Brimstones. Local manufacturers." Grim muttered 'umm' and 'ahh' and put on the handbrake. "Not important."

Marge laughed and clapped her hands. "He never gets that right. You'd think he would for all the times he's made this trip."

Gripping their envelopes, people stood as the windows on the bus went from blacked out to clear.

"Alright!" Grim stood. "Thank you, Marge." He pulled his pocket watch out, glanced at it, then opened the door when a tall woman wearing a full-length leather jacket over jeans and riding boots banged on the glass and tapped her wrist.

"What part of 'I've got plans. Don't be late.' don't you get?" The woman turned around and stalked up a cobbled path leading to a three-story building that looked like it had been airlifted from London's financial district, all pillars, wide stairs, and gargoyles.

Grim turned to his passengers. "Not an ideal welcome, I get that. But don't worry. You'll all be fine. Off the bus. Follow the mean lady. Her name is Karma. Yes, the one and only. She's my sister, so I know her bite is worse than her bark. Just do what she says."

No one moved. Billamy 'Call me Bill' gripped Harry's hand.

Hot desert air mingled with the stench of rotting river water filled the bus. Harry covered his nose and searched for a way out that didn't include going through that door.

They were parked in a mall-sized parking lot with no other vehicles in sight. To the left of the bus was rolling water littered with dead fish, tin cans, and soggy newspaper. In front of the bus stood the three-story, sandstone building. To the right of the bus, beyond the empty parking lot, was a flat, pale, bleached desert punctuated with nothing but a single, crimson lollipop sign hinting at their location: *Terminal*.

Grim smiled for a moment then let it drop like it was more hassle than it was worth. "Alright, folks." He unbuttoned his jacket, dabbed his head with the hanky, and shifted from foot to foot like the boots on his feet were a size too tight. "No, this is not Hell. Please forget the fairytales you've been told. That desert isn't a playground either, so stay out of it. This is Port Harker. It's the border town between life and death. You've all been here before one time or another. I know it's unfamiliar. It won't take long before memories of previous visits come back."

Grim cleared his throat again and pointed towards the building ahead of the bus.

This time, Harry noticed an arch that created an entrance to the docks, making Port Harker decidedly more like a port than it did before. No more comforting, but certainly more official.

With Billamy still holding tight, Harry dug his free hand into his dressing gown pocket and, for a moment, became aware of how soft the inside of his slippers were. He closed his eyes and let himself feel the warmth, then took another breath and stared up at the arch, which looked to be made out of every rock ever created, including more breeze blocks than should legally be allowed in one place. By contrast, the gates at the foot of that arch consisted of two Victorian-inspired wrought iron affairs that looked like they'd come off their hinges if anyone tried to close them. All design and no function, a toddler could have climbed over them if there were jellybeans on the other side. Inscribed on the gates were the words "Better Luck Next Time."

Grimmer tried the smile again. It lasted a little longer than the first attempt then vanished when he glanced out the window behind Harry. Harry followed the gaze. So did everyone else.

A wooden boat with rows of thin metal benches from bow to stern pulled up against a splintered, half-sunk pier. The middle of the boat was punctuated by a small wood shack. Less than a shack, Harry thought, and more like a roof on four stilts with half-constructed walls and a gap for a door.

Steering the boat from inside the shack was a sweaty-looking man dressed in green waders, oil-streaked dungarees, and a red checked shirt. The man picked up what looked to Harry to be a limb of some sort and threw it overboard where it burst into flames and sank.

Alicia Sascoona let out a shriek. "This *is* Hell! We're all going to Hell!" She ran down the aisle, tripped just before she reached Grim, and fell and smacked her head on the carpet before passing out.

Grim sighed. "It's not Hell. Damn it. This is why keeping to schedule is important."

Harry was sure Grim looked his way.

"As I just said," Grim continued, "Quite clearly, I thought. This is the *border town* between life and death. What happens to you here has not yet been decided. And Hell isn't what you think anyway. If you want to enjoy your stay, do yourself a favour and forget everything you think you know." Grim closed his eyes for a moment like he was trying to gather himself. The woman on the floor at his feet came round, shrieked, and fainted again.

Leaving her where she lay and ignoring Karma waving her arms telling him to get on with it, Grim wove through the seats, resting a hand on people's shoulders as he went. "That's just Charon on his boat messing around. You all have tickets. Please, don't panic."

Someone behind Harry gasped. "Oh, my God. What's he doing? Is that an arm?"

"It's nothing!" Grim covered his face with both hands. "Ignore him. He's being an idiot. Attention. Your attention, please!"

Grim reached up, pressed a button on the ceiling, and the windows went black.

Silence.

All faces turned to Grim.

"As I said, welcome to Port Harker. You all have your tickets. My sister, Karma… Yes, Mr. Bezuiz, *the* Karma, will lead you to the courthouse. Charon will take you into town after you've met the judge. Take a breath. Get off the bus. You're all going to be alright. One at a time, please. That's it, Mr. Shivaski. You can do it. Marge? Give him a hand, will you?"

A middle-aged man shaking so hard he could hardly stand gripped Marge's arm, and the two left the bus and joined Karma on the stone path outside.

"You see? That's how you do it." Grim smiled. "That's it. One at a time. No tip required, Agnus. Very kind, but not necessary. Watch the step, Ms. Windrow. Watch where you're…ouch. It's alright. Stand up and keep going. Mr. Bezuiz. That's it. Off you go. Left, Hector. I said… Left. Join Karma on the path. No… Not a good idea. Dammit. We have a runner! There's always one…"

Harry and Billamy leaned forward to get a good look out the door and watched Hector D. Bezuiz head into the desert then turn and sprint back towards the Port Harker gate when a flock of raging geese blocked his path and herded him back to Karma.

"And there you go, Mr. Bezuiz. Good job."

A ruddy-cheeked, rotund woman with curlers in her hair paused at the first step. "I thought dogs guarded the gates of Hell."

"Geese are far more effective, Mrs. Loola. And as I've already said, this isn't…forget it."

A young man joined Mrs. Loola on the step. Grimmer grinned and shook the man by the hand.

"Ricardo Muiz Lavoova Dove. Loved your music. You did great work this time round."

The man grinned and stood up straight for a moment. "Does that mean…"

"It means nothing, I'm afraid. Except, yours might be cooked." Grim chuckled, pointed to the geese, then wiped the smile off his face as tears welled in the musician's eyes. "No, no. Bad joke. Too soon? Apologies. It's alright. You're going to be fine. That's it. Down the stairs. No, your ex-wife isn't here… Oh, that's good news? Alright. Glad I could help."

Soul after soul, one at a time, everyone left the bus until finally…

"Harry?"

Harry looked up but didn't move.

"Mr. Blunt. It's time to go."

Harry shook his head and stayed where he was. "Why did you say what you said?"

Grim leaned against the back of a seat. "What did I say?"

"Just before I got on the bus, I said, '*Do you see my baby girl,*' and you said, '*Sadly, I do.*' Sadly. What did you mean by that?"

"It's not my place to discuss your case, Harry."

Inside, the bus was still and quiet. Outside, the geese squawked, Charon swore, Karma told someone to button it, and the people lining up behind her either laughed, cried, or screamed as body parts surfaced, sizzled, and sank in the river.

Harry rubbed his fingers along the edge of the envelope. "What did I do wrong? Do you know what's in here?"

Grimmer nodded.

Harry studied the smooth, dark skin of Grimmer's face, the high sheen of his head, and frowned when he saw a softness in Reaper's eyes.

"You said we'd all be alright."

"I lied."

"You can do that?"

"I'm Death. These are the gates to the afterlife. Literally my front door. I can pretty much do what I like."

"Can you send me back?"

Grimmer shook his head and sighed. "There's always one who has to run, one who has to deny it's happening at all, and one who wants to go back. I just do the transport, Harry. My job is to get you here."

Harry looked out the window. White, barren desert sand stretched beyond what he could see. "I've been here before?"

Grimmer followed Harry's gaze and pointed out over the eternal desert. "There's no water, no food, no end. Just a wind whipping up sand as high as the Port Harker lighthouse, the source of the sun itself. Still, people like Hector will risk that over the courthouse or

Charon's boat ride down the Styx. Yes, you've been here before."

"Why? I lived a good life. After my wife died, I focused all my attention on keeping my kids safe. Rainey was only a year old, you know. The boys were nine and eleven. I was a single dad. I helped people. I worked hard. I didn't steal, or cheat, or kill, or even get a single speeding ticket. I got a parking ticket once."

Grimmer frowned. "I'm not the one you should be pleading your case to."

"Then who?"

Harry didn't move as Grimmer leaned in close and looked so deep into his eyes that his soul felt naked. "What does Rainey want to do with her life? What's her purpose?"

Harry said nothing. Grimmer's eyes were rich and dark, bright and black all at once. They laughed and cried in equal measure. They held onto Harry and didn't let go.

"She's still working that out. She's young. Only 24." Harry swallowed then blinked tears out of his eyes, his breath tight in his chest, refusing to leave. "She has everything she needs. I gave her everything. She's alright."

"Exactly. So, do you understand?"

"No, bloody hell!" Harry pressed his lips tight shut. "Pardon my language. I don't understand."

"I guess that's why you're here." Grimmer walked to the front of the bus and down the stairs. "Karma's waiting. You don't want to annoy her. Good luck, Harry. It really is time to go."

Harry followed Grimmer off the bus, but by the time his foot hit hot tarmac dusted with scorched desert sand, Grim was gone.

▼

From a dune deep in the desert, Grim watched Harry search around and under the bus for him. The paisley dressing gown flapping in the wind, the man's thin ankles getting whipped by the sand and Harry not even noticing.

"With me!" Karma shouted. "Or it's the geese."

Harry turned to the desert and threw his arms in the air. "How am I supposed to fix things if I don't know what I did wrong?"

Grim pulled an old, battered phone from his pocket and dialled. After four rings, an answer service kicked in. *Leave a message* was all it said, so Grim did: "Harry Blunt is back."

HARRY IN COURT

Last in line and feeling like invisible eyes were peeling the skin off his body to see what was inside, Harry took it upon himself to look back every few seconds and monitor the birds, all thirteen of them. When they stretched their necks high and their wings wide, they were easily twice as tall as he was. Black eyes with small, yellow pupils gave them a deranged air a little like a sociopath with a belly full of brownies; violence interrupted by a craving for Cheetos.

"Keep up." Karma strode ahead without looking back. "If you get lost out here, no one will come looking."

Ahead of Harry, Hector D. Bezuiz sobbed. "Mami, perdóname por el tazón roto, y la galleta robada, y…" Hector turned to Harry.

"I don't understand you. I'm sorry."

"I ask forgiveness. You see where we are, no? Judgement! I beg my mother for forgiveness for the things I break and the food I steal. I beg of mercy…"

Ignoring the sweat dripping down his back and soaking into his dressing gown at the base of his spine, Harry squeezed the man's shoulder. "You'll be okay, Hector."

The man gripped Harry's hand. "How you know?" he whispered, keeping his eyes fixed on Karma. "We know nothing. This is not the thing I was told. I was told of angels waiting. St. Peter. Mi madre. Mi padre. Not this…this…"

Hector stretched his hand out into the desert to demonstrate the degree of "not this" he meant then screamed when a goose leaned over Harry's shoulder and pecked at his outstretched palm, hissing when it found the palm empty.

Hector stared up at the black-and-yellow-eyed bird, took three gasping breaths, then screamed. "Run!"

Harry wasn't sure if it was Hector's scream that triggered the stampede or the goose rearing up and flapping its wings, sending swirls of hot sand into the air. One moment, 188 people were walking in a line behind Karma. The next, 186 of those souls were shoving, scratching, and tripping over each other to get through the courthouse doors.

Marge threw her head back and laughed. Karma swore. The only reason Harry hadn't joined the race for safety was because one of his slippers had come off, and no way in hell was he going to go anywhere with one foot bare. He had standards.

"You got a problem, Harry?" Karma called over her shoulder.

The goose stretched out its wing so wide and so fast that it felt to Harry like a whirlwind was forming around them. Harry gripped one end of his slipper. The damn bird gripped the other.

"Nothing I can't handle."

"Ask the goose to let go. His name's Oscar."

The goose blinked.

Karma shrugged. "Ask and you shall receive. Isn't that how it goes? Ask nicely. They're sensitive."

Harry tightened his grip. "Oscar." The goose hissed. "Can I have my slipper? Please?"

In one movement, Oscar jerked his head back, flapped his wings, and swallowed Harry's right slipper whole.

Harry threw his hands in the air and turned on Karma. "You said, ask and you shall receive!"

Karma laughed, put her long arm around Harry's shoulders, and led him hobbling into the courthouse. "Since when has that ever worked? But I like that you tried."

Pressing his hands together so hard his joints clicked, Harry stuck as close to Karma as the thickening crowd allowed. The people on the bus had all been paired up with what appeared to be lawyers dressed in flowing black robes, a few even wearing perukes, all curled, powdered, and white.

The cool that should have come from the marble walls and floors of the courthouse had been taken over with body heat, thick, twitching, and tense.

"I don't understand." Harry stood tall so his whisper could reach Karma's ear. "If we're all dead, why do we still have bodies?"

"Bodies are easier to track and trace. Souls are slippery little bastards. Like life, Mr. Blunt, your perception of yourself is an illusion." Karma squeezed Harry's shoulder and increased her pace to a fast walk. "You're with me. Stay close."

Harry ran after Karma, who strode down a wide corridor lined with statues and portraits of smiling men and women holding up small trophies. Harry spotted Shakespeare, Genghis Khan, Gandhi, Agatha Christie, Nelson Mandela, and Rosa Parks before being pulled along by the crowd, which parted to allow Karma a clear path and closed immediately behind her, leaving

Harry to push and shove his way through. "Ms. Karma!"

Pressed on all sides, Harry navigated his way through the crowd of lawyers and the newly deceased, all still dressed, like Harry, in what they died in, and followed where he thought his escort went. The closer Harry got to a narrow glass door at the end of the corridor, the thicker the crowd became.

"Judge Cammie Sweet's presiding," a young lawyer with chocolate stains down his front muttered.

"She in a bad mood? If she is…" Another lawyer tied her hair back in a tight bun.

"She's been in a mood for months. Her and Boss-Lady Betuine are at it again."

"Is that what the boss is calling herself these days? I thought it was Queen Betuine. She had some soul pick up Lego bricks with bare feet in the dark for calling her Boss-Lady."

"I heard she threw someone in the Styx for calling her Queen."

"Best to steer…"

Harry squealed when a hand reached through the crowd and grabbed his dressing gown collar. "I said," Karma pulled him to her, "stay close."

Pressed up against Karma's back, Harry shuffled through the narrow door and into the courtroom already packed full of legal puffs and their clients.

The air, thick with the smell of fresh-baked cake and hot coffee, helped Harry take a breath, close his eyes, and remember the day Rainey baked her first batch of cupcakes. For a moment, the pressing, the shoving, the whispers, and the nudges faded, and he was in the kitchen with all three kids. Ben had put the fire out, Zach had thrown the pan into the garden, and 8-year-old Rainey had decided baking just wasn't her thing. They all ended up at the local pub for supper that night, full on pie and pudding.

"Harry Blunt."

Harry jumped then let himself be shuffled to the front of the courtroom.

Judge Cammie Sweet was dressed in an auburn kaftan, wore enough beads around her neck to own Mardi Gras, and had a green and yellow turban piled high on her head. She licked white frosting off her fingertips and sipped a rich, black espresso from a tiny porcelain cup.

No one spoke. Everyone waited.

"Well, well, Mr. Blunt." The judge flicked a smile at Harry that died just beneath her nose. "Welcome back."

Harry stared at the judge.

"How do you plead?"

"Guilty," Karma said and handed a bored-looking clerk Harry's envelope.

"Ahhh…" Harry patted his dressing gown pocket. He was sure that's where he'd put the envelope. He looked up at Karma then at the judge. Guilty? Of what? He ran through the highlight reel of his life and landed on exactly three things he felt guilty about. One, breaking a vase when he was eight; two, hiding the pieces of that broken vase under an old sofa; three, blaming the dog when the pieces were found. Then, he dismissed the series of mini crimes because the vase had been worthless and ugly.

When he thought about it now, he felt rather proud. Breaking that vase was the moment he got interested in antiques. It's how he managed to invest and accumulate the wealth he did. It's how he supported his family and gave them security that would see them through the rest of their lives, and if they were careful, the next generation too.

The judge opened the envelope, pulled out a single sheet of paper, balanced orange-tinted glasses on her nose, read, then glanced at Harry. "Do you understand the charges?"

Harry looked at Karma, who shrugged. "Don't look at me."

He blinked and squeezed his hands into tight balls. Then, he cleared his throat. "I don't understand," he said and felt his face burn hot and scarlet.

"I'm right here, Mr. Blunt. No need to shout."

Harry tried again. "I don't know what the charges are. I actually don't know anything. If someone could explain."

Someone chuckled at the back of the courthouse. The judge raised a finger and silence fell. She nudged her glasses down her nose and looked over them at Harry then spread the page out in front of her.

"Harry Samual Blunt," she read, "is hereby sentenced to 80 years in the 12th Circle of H.E.L.L - Headquarters for the Education for Life Lessons - for interfering with NDAPOAS - The Natural Development And Progress Of Another Soul - Under Act 271.5.4 Paragraphs 8.3.7 which states: No one soul should, must, can, is allowed or has the right to interfere with the natural progress, potential, and development of another…"

"80 years in Hell?"

"H.E.L.L.," the judge corrected. "Headquarters…"

Harry glanced up at Karma. "Education for what? Excuse me? What exact education do I need?" Harry pulled his dressing gown tight around his body, took a step towards the judge's bench, then glanced down at his bare foot and stepped back. He stood up straight. "That's unreasonable." He looked up at Karma, who closed her eyes and shook her head. "Isn't that unreasonable?"

"Make that 84 years for interrupting the judge."

"But this is crazy! That's a whole lifetime."

"87 years for questioning the judge's mental health."

"I want to speak to the boss. Boss-Lady Bet…Bet…er?"

A gasp filled the courthouse.

"Last chance, Mr. Blunt," the judge murmured.

Karma gripped Harry's arm. "The next words out of your mouth had better be *Thank you, Your Honour*."

"I don't..."

The judge banged her gavel down so hard her coffee spilled. "Next!"

Like Chinese squares, Harry found himself jostled and nudged until he was back in the corridor outside the courtroom.

"What just happened?"

Harry's remaining non-slip slipper failed him, and he slipped on the smooth tile. Karma's grip saved him from landing on his knees.

"You questioned the judge, you idiot."

"Not that. The charges. What do they mean?"

"You broke Rainey," Karma hissed in his ear and dragged him through the crowd.

"I did no such thing."

Out the courthouse and back in the desert heat, Karma let go of Harry. "You've committed the cardinal sin, Harry."

"I've never killed anyone in my life!"

"You might as well have. You've been charged with Interfering With The Natural Development And Progress Of Another Soul. NDAPOAS. There's no greater crime."

Harry covered his ears and closed his eyes. He needed to block out the light and shut out the noise. "I can't think here. I don't understand."

Standing on the front steps of the courthouse with the geese looking on, Karma stopped and forced the crowd to weave around them. She pulled Harry's hands away from his ears to make sure he heard every word. "You coddled Rainey to the degree that she's incapable of and unwilling to do any damn thing for herself. Anything. I'm not supposed to tell you this, but you've pissed me off. Rainey's been recalled."

"What do you mean, recalled? She's not a toaster."

"She's less than a toaster, Harry. She's not even that useful. Powers that be have decided that she's so pointless that her presence in Life could have a detrimental effect on others. She's going to be dead in three days, and when she gets here, she won't even get a court hearing. She's got a one-way ticket to the TV room."

"I don't…what?"

"Oblivion, Harry. The real end. Over. Kaput. What part of *recalled* don't you get? She gets to watch reruns of old game shows while her soul dwindles to nothing and she disappears, never to exist again."

"Purgatory?"

Karma stretched her arms above her and roared at the sky. The geese answered. "No, Harry. Purgatory is the waiting room you get to sit in after you've finished your education here and before your new life. You get tea and fricken biscuits there. The TV room is the absolute end of all existence."

"Where's Heaven? Can't she just go there?"

Karma shook her head. "No one except maybe our completely insane mayor, queen, boss-lady, or whatever she's calling herself today knows where that is, Harry."

"Who's the mayor? Can she fix this? Can she do something about this?"

Karma handed Harry his envelope. "Good luck, Harry."

▼

Karma watched Harry trip and stumble to Charon's boat. His remaining slipper fell off. He crawled on hands and knees to save it, but the geese got it first. They ripped it to pieces, ate most of it, and let the rest vanish in the wind.

"You can't do that!" Harry screamed.

Karma was sure he wasn't yelling at the geese or talking about his slipper.

Her phone chirped in her jacket pocket.

"How did he do?" Grim asked.

Karma watched the boatman put a blue stamp of a writhing eel on Harry's wrist. The type of stamp you get when you go to a museum, or a fancy bar, or a nightclub. Except, those stamps don't sink into skin and imprint on the soul.

One by one, the other souls, all sentenced to a lesser degree than Harry, wandered out the courtroom and to the boat. One by one, they all got the same stamp on their wrists and clambered aboard, all with questions, none getting answers.

"He doesn't get it," Karma finally said.

"This is his last chance."

"You aren't responsible, Grimmer. Free will exists for a reason. Hang on."

Karma watched Charon haul the last souls onto his boat, start the engine, and shove away from the dock into the middle of the Styx. She watched Harry stand up.

"No!" Harry yelled above the roar of the engine and the chopping waters of the river. "I'm not going anywhere with you. I want to see the mayor. I want to see the person in charge. Betu…Betta…Whatever the bloody hell her name is! Let me off this boat this instant!"

Karma covered her eyes. "I swear, humans don't learn." She opened them just in time to see Charon lift Harry off his feet and throw him overboard.

THE SWIM

Harry wasn't sure why he thought the water would be hot. It wasn't. It was lung-clenching, gasp-inducing, bladder-assaulting cold. With eyes squeezed shut and arms thrashing, he surfaced and blinked in time to see the boat disappear into a tunnel. Someone in the boat screamed. Charon guffawed. Then silence. Just lapping waves and a rumble from somewhere Harry couldn't pinpoint.

His body adjusting to the cold, Harry spat out the taste of salty ocean water.

From the middle of the river, the water wasn't black, filthy, or littered. There were no body parts or eels. It was clear, and blue, and calm. Fact is, the longer he stayed, the more comfortable it got. Warm almost, like a swimming pool on a sunny day.

He floated on his back just long enough to catch his breath, then he swam in a small circle and looked around him. Both shores were an equal distance away. To the right was the dock, splintered and rotting, tilting into the water like a chair with a missing leg. To the left was a cliff that disappeared into a thick bank of black clouds. Rain tried to fall, but heat from somewhere turned it to mist before it hit Harry's face. It wasn't unpleasant.

The cliff goes nowhere. Get back to the dock.

Harry started to swim, but all the lessons he'd had as a kid, the swimming clubs, the daily laps he'd committed to until illness made him too weak to do anything except float, did nothing for him. No matter how hard he kicked his feet or which stroke he used to pull himself through the water, he stayed in place.

Currents and tides. Right. Should have expected that. Something touched his leg. *Please let that be a log.* Something nudged his foot. Rough and spongy. Harry looked down into the clear water. Nothing there, not even a bottom. *Dear Lord, how deep does this go?*

The thing that touched his foot touched it again. Just a tap, like it was working out what Harry was.

Harry dipped his head under the water again, swallowed a mouthful, and choked on what felt like a piece of grass. A weed maybe? He coughed it up and spat it out.

Just a bit of grass. Harry blinked.

The grass wriggled and swam away.

Shore. Swim. Swim to shore. Just get out. Swim!

That's what he was screaming in his head, but he knew no sound was coming out because he was already a foot underwater and sinking fast, caught in a current that felt like a fist around his body.

Don't struggle against the water, Baby. That's what he'd said to Rainey during her one and only swimming lesson. She was six.

Harry closed his eyes. The sun was hot and bright that day. The boys were thrashing and splashing in the big pool. Harry was in the baby pool with Rainey. "Let the water carry you and hold you," he'd said.

Rainey hated it. She didn't like getting her face or her hair wet. How can a six-year-old not like swimming? Harry had laughed and held her. Feeling her tiny arms squeeze his neck was pure heaven. Absolute bliss. She'd gripped his neck and refused to let go. Even when the boys joined in and tried to make a game of it, she still wouldn't let go. In the end, Harry had carried her out the water, dried her, and they'd gone for ice cream while the boys kept playing.

Just Harry and his baby girl. She'd had strawberry ripple. He'd had vanilla. She'd had two flakes. He'd had one. She'd dropped half hers on the table, so Harry had given her his with added chocolate sauce. They never went back to the pool. The boys did almost every week through that summer. Not Rainey.

Harry opened his eyes. *Oh, good Lord.* Harry ran out of air as his body screamed for release. *Rainey can't swim.*

In that moment, the grip became a shove, and Harry breached the surface for just long enough to take a single breath before the current dragged him down again.

This time, the water was dark and cold, and something moved around him that he couldn't see. It touched him here and there, and nudged, and pulled. It circled his shin like a leg-iron from one of those old, black-and-white prison movies his mother liked to watch.

Not again. Please, not again. Harry curled into a ball and held himself close.

Memories. They had to be memories. Just memories. Let them pass. Let them go.

But those memories felt like hands on his body.

The day his father lost everything; his job, their home, every penny they had. One moment Harry had a bed to sleep in. The next, he was sharing the backseat of their station wagon with his mum. Then, a bedroom with his cousin. Then, a motel with a stranger.

Let the water carry you. Harry covered his face with his hands and held his nose and mouth shut. *It'll let you up. It always does. Just memories. Nothing's real. Nothing happened.*

The fist around his body became a hand on his leg and Harry screamed, pulling water into his lungs and his belly. Even his bones seemed to fill up, and he sank.

His father's words. The day after his mother overdosed, and they all ended up in hospital. *"I'll work things out, my boy. It's what the Blunt family does. We work things out. Just breathe. Relax."*

Harry breathed.

I must be dead.

Then, he laughed.

I am dead!

He opened his eyes and looked around him. The current had slowed. The water was clear. His feet rested on a soft, sandy riverbed. A koi swam by and ignored him.

I'll work things out. That's what the Blunt family does.

Harry looked up. There was movement on the surface above him like fish at feeding time. Hundreds of them, maybe thousands, all darting and thrashing, grabbing and snatching.

Only way is up, Harry.

Those were the exact words his dad used the night his mother almost died. From that moment, Harry watched the most determined man he knew rebuild the family business, the family home, and the family itself. The man built a legacy. The day he died, he was still building.

Only way is up, Harry. Always.

Harry swam.

Without a current holding onto him, Harry ploughed through the water and through the increasing mass of hungry fish, grabbing at bits of food. He didn't stop until his head breached the surface.

"There's someone there! That's a person! Grab his hand."

Harry blinked water out his eyes as a dozen strangers reached towards him, gripped his arms, and heaved. They hauled on his shoulders, then his body, then his legs and didn't let go until Harry was out of the water, lying flat on his belly, choking up weeds and one small fish.

Harry pressed his hands down on warm, solid, dry wood and took a real breath.

"I'm going to sort this out," he whispered. "I will fix this, whatever it takes."

"What he say?" Someone knelt beside him. "Hey. Harry. Is me. Hector. We thought you be eaten, man. Eaten by dat freaky eel. But here you are. He make it!

This Harry Blunt. He swim the river! Drink on me, my man."

Hector D. Bezuiz hauled Harry to his feet and handed him a shot glass. "Drink. It fire up belly to leave you floaty light." Hector threw his arms in the air. "Welcome Port Harker!"

Every soul packed into the ramshackle, timber-built bar cheered. Harry sipped and let the warmth of exceptionally and unexpectedly fine brandy course through his limbs. He put the glass down and glanced at the bottle: Betuine Gold. Harry hadn't heard of it.

"Who's Bet…?"

A country band huddled around glass-filled tables started to play honky-tonk, and Harry's question was lost in the whoops and hollers.

He picked up the glass that had been refilled without him noticing and took another sip and a breath.

The interior of the bar was something Harry would have expected to see in an old Wild West movie. All-wood walls, beams, and stairs made up the three levels of the place. The second and third floors were balconies looking down on the main bar, each with doorways heading to what Harry assumed were private rooms. Round tables littered the ground floor where he stood, each one filled with people drinking, laughing, playing some game with stones Harry had never seen, and poker with cards where a cartoon red devil replaced the King, Queen, Jack, and Joker.

The bar itself was a circle in the middle of the room. The man behind the bar was bigger than any man Harry had ever seen. No matter how drunk someone was, they suddenly sobered and remembered their manners when they approached the bar to order another drink that no one seemed to pay for.

"I need to get out of here. Hector. No more drinking. Just…"

"We pull you out river, bro. You should see what we saw. First is just wild fish and crazy. Then we see you. Swimming like demon after you. I thought, for sure. This is devil. Coming up to take our souls. Then, brother. I see your face, and I say to everyone! Is Harry!"

The crowd raised their glasses and cheered again. "Is HARRY!"

Harry squeezed water out his dressing gown, soaking the floor around him, and flung a wriggling thing out of his pocket.

The barman, polishing glasses only to fill them again, called over his shoulder. "Jankins! Get a towel for the man."

A young man looking like he was getting away with a jewel heist leapt over the bar with a towel in one hand and an empty tray in the other. He handed Harry the towel, darted around the bar gathering empty glasses, then, like he was in a hurry to get things done, he returned to Harry and grabbed the towel back.

"I'm not done," Harry snapped. He didn't mean to. It just came out.

The young man laughed like Harry had just told him a brand-new joke. He grabbed the towel again.

Harry grabbed it back.

The boy pulled.

Harry pushed.

For a moment, time between Harry and the boy Jankins seemed to pause. Jankins held one end of the towel. Harry held the other.

"Don't…," Jankins said, leaning back on one foot, searching around for something to hold onto.

Harry let go.

With a look of despair and resignation, the boy fell through the double doors leading out of the bar…and disappeared.

The crowd gasped and fell silent.

No one except the barman moved. Harry wouldn't have minded, but the big man was heading straight for him. Without the bar between them, the man was taller and broader than Harry had first thought. A thick head of bird-nest hair gave him more than additional height; it created an air of unhinged insanity. Tattoos of dragons (or maybe eels?) wound around each arm, across his chest, and up his neck, disappearing into a thick, tangled beard.

"What the hell just happened?" the barman barked, and everyone took a step back.

"He… I…" Harry picked up the towel, folded it, and held it up to the barman like an offering. "He had given me a towel. I was still using it, and he tried to take it away."

"So, you shoved him. You shoved him *through a door.*"

Harry refolded the towel into a neat square, put it on a small, round table, and glanced at the door in question. People milled about on both sides of the doorway. "I just…I don't know where he went. He…did you see that?" He turned to the crowd. They averted their eyes. Harry turned back to the barman. "It wasn't intentional. Honestly."

The barman looked at Harry like he was a problem to solve or an inconvenience to get rid of and he couldn't decide which.

Harry looked around the room. "I'm sorry. I just…"

"Oh, Harry." Hector shook his head. "Sending Jankins through the door was not nice. Not kind."

Harry picked up the towel again and handed it to the barman. "I didn't know…where did he go? I mean…what can I do?"

The barman grabbed the towel and took a step toward Harry. Harry took a step back. He looked back into the water. The fish weren't koi. These ones had rows of polished, sharp teeth. The barman opened the towel and shook it like he was daring Harry to charge at him. The barman lunged. Harry fell back. The barman wrapped the towel around Harry's neck, pulled him into a schoolboy headlock, and rubbed Harry's head until he could hardly breathe.

Like a pressure valve had been released, every soul in the bar laughed, and Harry was the punchline.

"Damn fool was pressing his luck anyway." The barman released Harry and draped the towel over his shoulders. "Welcome to Mink's Tail Tavern, my friend. Quite an entrance you made. Take a seat. Name's Barkmore Adams. Folks around here call me Barky. First round's on me."

"I'm sorry about Jankins."

"Don't be. You're taking his place."

"Taking his place doing what?"

"He was my best delivery boy."

"Delivering what?"

Barkmore Adams lifted a wooden crate of foiled packages onto the bar. "Best ribs in Port Harker."

Harry dropped the towel onto the bar. "I can't do that. I have to get out of here."

"Out of where, Harry?"

"This place. Port Harker. I need to get back to my life. I've got things I have to fix."

Barky reached up to a brass bell over his head and rang it. The bar cheered, "No way back! No way back!"

Harry shook his head. "You don't understand. My daughter is going to die in three days."

"That's great! Everyone finds their way here sooner or later. You will be halfway through your seven days. You'll have plenty of time to catch up."

"Seven days?"

"Everyone gets seven days between judgement and the next thing."

"The next thing?"

"Bloody hell, Harry. Did no one explain anything to you?" Barkmore leaned over the bar, put his hand around the back of Harry's neck, and pulled him close. "If you've lived an epic previous life, you get seven days in Port Harker, choose your next life, and off you go. If you've screwed up, you get seven days in Port Harker, then you start your sentence. Those beautiful, seven days? Anything you like. Zero consequences. No record. Some people call it heaven. It's not, but you can believe what you like."

"Rainey's not getting seven days of anything. She's getting a ticket to the TV room."

The crowd fell silent again. This time, everyone put their glasses down and bowed their heads.

"No!" Harry released himself from Barkmore's grip, picked up a shot glass, drank it in one, and slammed it onto the bar. "This won't happen. I'm going to go back and fix it. I just need to know how."

Barky reached up to the bell and rang it again.

The bar erupted, "No way back! No way back!"

"And you owe me deliveries." Barkmore Adams stacked another pack of steaming ribs onto the pile. "When you get back, I'll have the next box ready."

"What happened to Jankins?"

"You sent him to H.E.L.L., Harry. Congratulations. You're a proper bastard. Now, pick up the box and go."

Harry stared at the doorway through which Jankins had just vanished and he was now expected to walk. "Does this door lead to Hell? Am I going to disappear when I walk through that door too?"

Harry searched the faces around him. People whispered between themselves. Not one of them would meet his eyes. Some covered their faces and turned around.

Barkmore Adams rubbed Harry's shoulders. "You won't know until you take the step, my man. Good luck."

"But…"

Barkmore shook his head. "If you make it back, we can talk."

Harry lifted the box weighing about what two bowling balls might weigh and stood at the doorway through which Jankins had vanished. He glanced back at Barkmore. The barman nodded a "Go with God" kind of nod. Part reverence, part pity.

"Where am I going to end up when I walk through this door? What happens?"

Barkmore shrugged.

Harry looked down at a boy around seven years old. The boy gripped Harry's dressing gown. "It's alright," he said. "We'll go together. It won't hurt. Much."

The crowd behind Harry was silent. All faces turned to the door and watched. The child blinked impossibly large eyes.

"What's your name?" Harry asked.

The boy smiled. "It doesn't matter."

"What happens next? Where did Jankins really go?"

"He started his sentence. Like going to jail. No one is really sure." The boy wiped his nose on Harry's dressing gown then looked up at him and blinked out a tear.

"I've got things to do," Harry said.

The boy reached up and patted Harry on the arm. "We all have things to do. Go through the door, Harry. You won't feel a thing. Follow the light."

Harry closed his eyes, held his breath, and took a step through the doorway.

When Harry opened his eyes again, the bar was still there, the crowd was still there, and the boy and Barkmore Adams were still there. Harry was still there, standing outside the bar on a wraparound porch that surrounded the tavern. Still holding the box, the crowd was still watching his every move.

For just one moment, there was silence. Then, the boy doubled up laughing, the bar cheered, and Barkmore Adams chuckled.

The boy tugged Harry's dressing gown. "Here's what you need to know," he said in a tone far older than his years. "You have seven days in Port Harker before your sentence. As soon as those seven days are up, the next door you walk through, no matter where it is, becomes the entrance to where you've been sentenced. Jankins had managed to avoid doorways for a month. A month! When you pushed him and he fell through those doors, he fell into the 8th Circle of Hell where he'll spend 27 years learning what it is to be a single mother of multiple children." The child patted Harry on the arm again. "Jankins would have walked through a door sooner or later, Harry. Guy was going for the record."

"What's the record?"

"Old Lady Collida. You'll see her in the streets. Crazy thing is, her sentence is only 26 years in the 3rd Circle. Lightweight, but she's managed to avoid doors for over 100 years. You'll know her when you see her."

"Barkmore could have told me all this."

The kid chuckled and turned back into the tavern. "He did. You just didn't listen."

Harry glanced back into the bar. Barkmore lined a dozen shot glasses in front of the kid. "Don't let those ribs go cold, Harry!"

"This is madness," Harry muttered and stepped onto the swinging rope bridge that linked the Mink's Tail

Tavern, which stood on impossibly thin stilts in the middle of the lake, to the shore.

▼

Barkmore leaned against the bar and polished glasses while Harry wobbled across the bridge, gripping the box of ribs under his arm.

"How am I supposed to know where to deliver the ribs?" Harry yelled.

"You always find what you need in Port Harker," Barkmore replied. "The place is weird that way."

"Will I find a way out?"

Barkmore ran the bell again and the crowd cheered, "No way out!"

The bar floor shook, and the building swayed on stilts that ran the depth of the lake and anchored in the bedrock that carried Port Harker itself. The wooden building, built back before Port Harker was even an idea in anyone's head, rattled and shook. Every man, woman, and child jumped up and down in time with a new beat the band had just picked up.

"Welcome to Port Harker!"

Glasses rose with the voices. Barkmore Adams ran his fingers through a beard that hadn't been trimmed in over five thousand years and topped the glasses up again.

THE ROAD TO BETUINE

Back on dry land, Harry followed a stone path away from the lake towards a narrow tunnel carved into a cliff that reared up ahead of him so high and so steep that it seemed more like a fortress designed to keep giants of the universe out than anything natural. Harry didn't follow the path because he knew where he was going; he followed it because it was the only way through the shoulder-high reeds that surrounded the lake. The path was manicured to the degree that it seemed rude not to walk it and ended, as all paths do, at the entrance of something. In this case, a tunnel at the foot of those cliffs.

Harry adjusted the box of ribs under his arms. "You always find what you need in Port Harker," he said out loud, just to hear the sound of something other than rustling reeds and lapping water. He could still see Mink's Tail Tavern in the middle of the lake, but it was like the sound had cancelled itself, like a TV on mute.

Harry faced the tunnel. "I have to get out of here."

He glanced back to the inn. Barkmore must have rung the bell again because everyone was jumping up and down, and unless Harry was imagining, they were all pointing at him.

"No way out," Harry said. "Sure. Maybe." And he stepped into the tunnel.

For a moment, darkness enveloped him. A comforting dark. The kind you see when you wake in the night, still tired, with things to do in the day that you're not quite ready for, only for the numbers on your bedside clock to tell you it's only just gone midnight. You have a whole night to sleep, so you bury yourself under the covers and let the world fade to black. That kind of comfort.

Then, like nightlights in a dream, the tunnel around Harry began to shimmer. The walls were sheer and curved into a domed ceiling high above him. As his eyes adjusted, he noticed an infinite number of tiny portholes in the wall. Each one had a little windowsill.

Every windowsill had a small, flickering candle. Some were long and standing tall, their flames shining bright, while others seemed to be burning on little more than the pool of melted wax around them. When one of those candles finally got so close to snuffing out that it seemed a miracle it was still burning, the porthole opened, a gnarled hand reached out and replaced it with a new, upstanding candle, lighting the new flame from the dying embers of the old one.

"Wall of Transition," a voice said from a window just above his head. "A new candle for every soul moving from one life to the next. Life to Port Harker and back to Life. Round and around we go." A head followed the voice and peered down at Harry. Harry gripped the box tight.

"Ohhhh." A thin man with teeth too big for his face grinned. "Tell me my order's in there."

He reached a hand down. Harry took a step back and rifled through the packages. Barkmore had written names on each one with a thick black pen, but most of the ink had sweated off.

"Put it this way," the toothy man said, keeping the grin fixed on his face. "Hand me my ribs or I'll snuff this candle out, right now."

"And that's supposed to scare me?"

"It'll scare the poor sap who drops dead for no reason."

Harry held the box up. "That's unnecessarily aggressive."

"It's called negotiation. I read about it once."

The man reached into the box, and a pack of ribs disappeared.

Harry stretched up and tried to see where the voice, the face, the hand, and one order of ribs had vanished to. "Where does this tunnel lead?"

Silence.

Perfect.

Harry squeezed through the tunnel, careful not to disturb a single flame, and increased his pace from careful to brisk when he saw a change in the light ahead of him. The light at the end of the tunnel was the entrance to a park, all trees, fountains, swing sets, and benches.

"Where is everyone?"

Harry squeezed the box of ribs to his chest and welcomed the warmth. He had a choice of not one but nine paths to take, all fanning like spokes on a second-hand bike from the tunnel exit. One path was made up of cobbles, another of loose stones, one of grass, and another of rocks and twigs. Only one looked like anything Harry would call a road, smooth tarmac, straight, with a line down the middle. Normal.

Harry closed his eyes for a moment. "One straight line," he said to no one because no one was there. "I just want to walk one straight, normal line."

He stepped onto the tarmac path, but within a few steps, it felt wrong. The path was too warm, and although it didn't look it, was slippery under his feet. He stepped off the path and onto cool grass.

"Rainey," he said without meaning to and smiled at the memory of the park by his house with the hill, the kids rolling down it. The only person who saw the dog poop in Rainey's path was Rainey herself. She screamed but had no control. The boys laughed about that for a week. Rainey didn't. It took a day in a bath, three visits to a hair salon, two stacks of pancakes, and a promise never to roll down hills again. So, they didn't. The smile on Harry's face faded. Never again, since that day, did Rainey roll down a hill.

Harry stepped off the grass and onto a cobbled path.

"My ribs in that box?" An old man on a unicycle wobbled by, reached into the box, and picked out a steaming bundle of foil. "Thanks, bud!" He disappeared into a forest Harry hadn't noticed.

Harry followed the man. Not because this man was the first soul he'd seen since the one in the tunnel but because there was noise in that direction. It was like a bubble had burst or the mute button had been switched off. There was life on the other side of that forest.

Harry scrambled through the trees expecting to feel the forest floor stab and prick his bare feet, but every step felt like he was running through soft grass until a root reached up, grabbed him, and tripped him up.

Thinking only to protect the foil packages, Harry twisted and landed on his back. From there, he looked up through the last few trees to see more people than he saw at the courthouse and the bar combined.

This wasn't a crowd. It was a clamour, chaos, and mess of humanity. A crowd like he'd never seen. Crowds upon crowds squeezed into a raucous market space. The kind you see around the world from Akar to India or Soho to Durban. He knew the crowd was thick because the words he heard most were, "Excuse me. Out the way. A little space if you don't mind!"

Harry stood up, checked the ribs were all still there, and took a step into the human stream only to be shoved against a wall by an old lady who looked like she'd just turned 112.

"Out the way, nugget head! I'm walking here. Ohhhhh, you got the ribs!"

She reached into the box and picked out a pack only to have them snatched out of her hand by the old man on the unicycle.

"Finders keepers, my Lady Collida." He whooped and tore a chunk of meat out the wrapping.

The Port Harker record holder for avoiding the start of her sentence, Lady Collida herself, squealed, picked up a cantaloupe from a basket at her feet, and threw it, hitting the man squarely on the back. He wobbled and fell into a barrel of tacks. She doubled up with a laugh that ended in, "Jackass!"

Leaving Lady Collida behind, Harry dodged around a tower of barrels filled with an amber liquid that guaranteed oblivion in just one glass and sank into a quieter lane with arches to the left and right that looked to Harry like they were part of an abandoned railway bridge.

He leaned against a wall and took a breath. "This is madness."

Each arch led to a cavernous interior. Some were filled with dry fish hanging off hooks from the ceiling. Others had cloth and clothing merchants touting woven wares. All had people weaving between the goods, talking, laughing, scrapping, bickering, bartering, eating, and drinking.

Harry paused at a store with *"Suits You Fine: Specialists in Tailored Suits, Cuffs, Collars, and Bow Ties"* printed in black and gold above the doorway. He glanced at his state of undress.

"That's mine, and his, and his, and the other hers." Four packs of ribs disappeared out of the box. "Thank you, kind sir!" Harry didn't even see who took them.

He took a step forward, focusing on nothing but the *Suits You Fine* store, and walked right in front of a rickshaw rider, sending her careering into a food stall, launching a domino effect that ended with a basket of peaches, six chickens, and the rider headfirst in a barrel of the amber liquid.

Harry fell backward, tripped over an alley cat slinking across the cobbled lane, dodged a bottle hurled from an upstairs window, and patted out a flame on his sleeve as he darted through sparks billowing from a glassblower's kiln.

He lifted the box of ribs high above his head. "Free ribs if anyone wants them!" he yelled over the noise of a brass band belting out the first four bars of William Tell's Overture. A gaggle of nuns inviting anyone to guess which cup the mouse was under (for a fee) paused their con and peered into the box.

"Ohhhhh no, Sister J. Not that one."

"Last one in the box, Sister M. Don't touch that one."

"Don't even look. That's Betuine's, Sister C. The madman is giving away Betuine Harker's ribs."

The nuns crossed their arms, pushing their bosoms up, emphasising their multiple chins. "Well, that's just plain madness."

"Betuine Harker?" Harry peered into the box. There was only one pack left. *Betuine Harker* was printed on the foil in black ink. "The mayor? The person who runs this place?"

"One and only," Sister J. said.

"Where is she? How can I get this to her? I mean," Harry straightened his dressing gown and slapped a thieving hand out of the box, "If I'm going to deliver this to Betuine Harker, how do I find her?"

Sister C. turned her attention to the three cups. She lifted one. A small, white mouse stood on its hind legs and raised its paws like it was begging for mercy. It got none. The nun trapped it in the cup. "How did you deliver the rest of your ribs?"

Harry shrugged. "I just walked, and people found me."

The nun grinned. "There you go then."

"There I go where then?"

"Just walk!"

Before Harry could ask a question that might actually elicit a useful answer, a crowd gathered around the nuns and placed bets on the whereabouts of the indentured mouse.

After only two close encounters, one with a fire-breathing juggler and another with an indignant pope, Harry rounded a corner and came to a narrow arch with a door so low he had to duck to get through. He stepped through and found himself in a small, abandoned square with nothing but a stone well in the middle.

For what seemed like the first time since he sat on the bus, Harry sat on the edge of the well and took a breath.

The smell of prime BBQ sauce wafted and faded as it does on food as it cools. "Bloody hell," he muttered and looked down the well when he heard a click and a whisper, a shuffle, and what he was sure was a sneeze. "Hello?"

"Hello?"

"Anyone down there?"

"Anyone down there?"

"This isn't funny. I've got a delivery for Betuine Harker?"

"This isn't funny… Are those my ribs? Are they cold? What part of *hot and fresh off the fire* don't you get?! Just drop them and get out of here. Unbelievable. UN-believeable. Where's Jankins? I like Jankins. Who the hell are you, and what the behoovis are you doing sitting on my well? MY well! That's mine! Get your butt off my well!"

Harry stood. "Miss Harker?"

"Mayor, to you."

"Mayor Harker."

"Call me Queen."

"Queen?" Harry took a step back from the well. "Ahh… Queen Harker. It's Harry Blunt."

"And I care why?"

"I'd like to talk. I'd like to talk to you."

"Everyone wants to talk to me. I'm famous."

"I know. Right. I know. You're the owner and CEO."

"And the mayor."

"And the mayor."

"Drop the ribs."

"If I bring them down, they'll be less likely to land in a pile on the floor."

"You saying I'm too stupid, weak, or blind to catch?"

"No! Not at all."

"Are you saying there's something wrong with being blind?"

Harry rubbed his face. "No. I just…I really need to talk to you."

"Are you happy, Harry Blunt?"

Harry paused. "As it happens. I'm not happy at all."

"That makes two of us. Fine. Bring them down. You have whiskey?"

"Ahhh. No?"

"I'm not sharing."

"Okay. That's okay."

Harry stuck the ribs in his dressing gown pocket and stepped into the well. Less than a dozen rungs down the stepladder, darkness folded around him so thick that it crawled into his flesh and seated just under his skin, making every hair on his arms feel like pinpricks.

There was light at the bottom of the well. Then, muttering.

"Excuse me?" He tried to look down. "Did you say something?"

▼

Betuine Harker frowned. She was good at hiding. Had been since she realised she was never going to get out of Port Harker. Trapped forever. Trapped for eternity. Trapped, and stuck, and a goddamn prisoner.

"I'm in charge," she whispered. "I'm the one in charge. I get to say how things go. Me! Lady Betuine. Queen B. Your Highness Honorship Dutchess King Betuine Harker the First and Only. Now, bow."

She dipped a deep curtsy to herself then looked up the well, watching what's-his-name stumble down. "Ribsy, ribsy, rib, rib, ribsy," she muttered. "I might eat him too."

"Excuse me?" The silly man peered down. "Did you say something?"

Betuine flicked a switch and turned off the lights. "Don't be mean," she murmured. "Give him one little bulb." She skipped into the dark, hid around a corner, and chuckled. "Gonna have me some fuuuuuun!"

THE DEAL

Warm gusts of air billowed past Harry from below, carrying smells of ripe manure with the occasional hint of honey.

Harry missed a step, dropped a foot, squealed, and gripped the rope ladder with both hands. "Oh, my God. Oh, my God. This place is going to kill me."

He took another step and found himself standing on solid ground.

A single lightbulb that looked like it'd struggle to light up a branch on a Christmas tree hovered above his head. He took a step into the tunnels. That light faded, and another one pulsed on a few feet ahead of him.

The dense smell of moss, dead and dry cockroaches, soil, and rancid oil filled his nostrils. He took another step forward into the next patch of light. He looked ahead and behind him. Darkness, thick and black. He took a step out of the light, and the next bulb flicked on.

Harry's gut churned, and for the first time since he arrived, he felt the urgent need to pee. *Can't very well piddle in the mayor's hallway.* Harry paused and focused on that strange, familiar, physical feeling until a breeze from somewhere caught his attention.

It was warm, not hot, and carried the smell of burned bacon and glue. Harry tightened the belt around his gown. Something feather-light touched his left leg. He flinched, stood on one foot for a moment, then leaned down and rubbed his ankle.

"What do you want to talk about?" a voice said from the dark. "Don't try to small talk con me. If I don't believe you, I'll have my wicked way with you. I know a liar when I see one. So, honest as you can. What do you want to talk about?"

Harry stood under a single, flickering bulb and peered into the dim. His gut clenched, his back dripped sweat, and his hands tingled. *Breathe*, he said to his lungs. He swallowed dusty spit. "I need to get back to Life."

"You and a billion others. No can do."

"I made mistakes, and my daughter shouldn't pay for that." There was silence for a while. "Mayor Harker?"

"Everyone makes mistakes, Harry. Everyone dies having not quite finished. That's the nature of the beast. If you do everything you need to do in one life, then what's the point of going back for another one? And ask anyone; going back for another round is way more fun than staying in the same one for too long. I should know."

Harry took a step out of the light. The bulb above him spluttered out. The dark pressed against his flesh and squeezed. A warm breeze carrying a tiny suggestion of lavender kissed Harry's neck, then moved on like he wasn't quite what it was looking for. "The thing is, Queen…"

"Your Royal Duchess."

"…Your Royal Duchess, is that my Rainey won't be getting another go."

A chuckle slid out the dark, twisted around Harry's heart, and slithered away. "The TV room. She'll like it. A sixty-six season soap. There's popcorn."

Harry didn't move. Couldn't. The dark beyond the halo of light created by the tiny bulb was too thick. Stepping into it was too much like diving into an ocean too deep to see the bottom and what might be lying in wait.

"She's got so much to offer. She just needs a little time. She needs more than three days."

"More time. More Life. More everything. It's all you humans want."

Harry glanced behind him. He swore Betuine Harker's voice moved around him like a wasp looking for a place to burrow.

"You have no idea what you have," she whispered. "You just want more of what you think you don't have. Ever wonder why you keep having to go back to Life? Over and over? Because you don't like to do the hard things, Harry Blunt. You don't take responsibility for anything."

Betuine's voice rose from whisper-quiet to preacher-loud. "You learn in baby steps, my son. Too slow." Her voice switched to coffee shop conversational. "Do you know it takes the average human seven lives to learn to be kind? Seven lives to learn the impact of a simple act of kindness. Twelve lives to learn what love really is. Twelve, Harry, and that's for the average soul. You've lived 17 lives, and all you've done is break the people you say you care about most. Break them to the point of destruction. Why should I give you more time? What can you possibly do in three days that you haven't done in 17 lifetimes?"

"17 lifetimes?"

"Focus. Harry."

"What can I do in three days? I don't know. I have to try."

"We all have to try, Harry. We're all stuck. We all need something."

The light above Harry's head flickered and went out. He drew air into his lungs. "What do *you* need?"

Silence.

"Your Royal…Queen…Miss Harker?"

"I heard you."

Harry shuffled his bare feet on the dusty stone. They were warm like the stones had been baking in the sun all day and had just started to cool at dusk. Harry swallowed what felt like a solid lump of grit in his throat and took a step forward. The next bulb above him flicked on.

Harry blinked. "Oh, my Lord," he gasped and took a step back into the dark.

In the halo of light stood a woman. Young. In appearance, no more than twenty-five, Harry thought. She had a soft, round face with bright eyes so blue they were almost purple. Her thick, black hair was tied in a messy knot on the top of her head and, on inspection, was littered with pencils, pens, two chopsticks, and a thin chocolate bar wrapped in green and silver foil. She was shorter than Harry by almost a foot and wore a flannel rabbit onesie, ears and all, and furry armadillo slippers.

"I like your dressing gown," she said. "Classic."

Harry ran a hand down the silk, paisley garment that, by now, was so stained and torn he was beginning to feel unkempt. "I like your…slippers. Cosy?"

"Very." Betuine glanced at Harry's pocket. "Them's my ribs?"

Harry nodded, reached into his pocket, and handed over the foil package. He watched as Betuine Harker, the mayor and CEO of the Afterlife, opened the foil package, pulled out a rib, licked off the sauce, and bit into the meat. "Hmmm, hmmmm, hmmmmm," she murmured and wiped dribble off her chin with her sleeve. "Hot, cold, or covered in dressing gown lint, no one anywhere does ribs better than Barky," she sighed.

Harry plastered what he hoped was a polite smile on his face, but it made his jaw ache, so he stopped trying. "So, you said everyone wants something. What do you want?"

Betuine took another bite. "I want to find my father so I can ask him why he deserted me. Why he disappeared on me. Why he left me with this mess." She used the rib to draw a circle above her head suggesting everything above her was included in the mess she found herself in. "I want to ask the man who was supposed to love me why he hates me so much. That's what I want, Harry."

"Er…father…you have a… Where is your father?"

Betuine lifted another rib to her nose and inhaled the scent. "Somewhere in Life."

"Can't you just go and find him? If you're the boss, can't you just go?"

Betuine gnawed on the rib. "Can't. Not while I'm the only one in charge of everything. I had one opportunity. One ticket. I used that 100 years after my bastard of a dad deserted me. Then, I decided I don't like people anyway. They're rude and insulting. No respect. They're lying, thieving, bullish, and unpredictable."

"Maybe you just caught them on a bad day?"

"No matter how bad your day is, it's no reason to drag anyone behind a horse, or burn them alive, or drown them, or stick spikes into their head. There are other ways to handle having a bad day."

"When were you last on earth?"

"1465. It was a Thursday. The moment I arrived, someone pushed me into a fireplace. I thought I'd made a mistake and arrived in the middle of some celebration, so I created another body and tried again. It took all of three days for the scheming bastards to drown me then hang me for good measure. I left that body for the last time when they lit a match on it. I came here and I vowed never to return. Not that I have a choice. That was my only pass."

"You were there during the witch trials. I guess when people saw you appear out of nowhere then reappear after they were sure you were dead, they thought you were a witch."

"Don't be an idiot. I used a different suit, and I'm not a witch." Betuine took a step forward. Harry took a step back. "And even if I was, what's wrong with that?"

"Nothing." Harry curled his toes against the stone in an effort to keep himself standing exactly where he was. "A lot has changed in Life since then."

"I don't care. People are people. Here, they do what they're told because they know I run things. Up there, they just didn't get it. Free will's not convenient. If I could, I'd make it illegal."

"So, you tried to tell the people you met in Life that you ran things?"

"I was as clear as I could be. I told them I was looking for my father, the original mayor of the Afterlife. I even described him. 60,000 years old but looked like 45. Dark hair, blue eyes. Tall. They looked at me like I was crazy. Worse than that, I knew them all. They'd all been through Port Harker. I'd done everything possible to help them do better in their next life. Because that's why I'm here. That's what I built."

A tear welled up in Betuine's eye. Harry took a step forward then stopped himself. She kept talking.

"I've worked hard, Harry Blunt. Before I joined the design team, this place was the hell and damnation you read in storybooks. People had no chance. Then, I took over and invented therapy and counselling. Hypnosis was my idea. I invented coffee makers. And where do you think the inspiration for vending machines came from? Me. I helped people. I still do. If someone struggles to respect women and mothers in one life, I show them the error of their ways, then I make them a mother of six in the next life. People learn fast. Everyone I met on my last trip to Life, I knew. I'd helped. They had no respect, Harry. No gratitude. It was hurtful."

"I guess the trouble is that most people in Life have an idea that a bearded, white guy runs things. They don't really know what you do. We aren't born with memories of…" Harry looked around him but saw only blackness, "…here."

Betuine nodded. "You have a point. I suppose that makes some sense. Hadn't thought of that." She chewed another rib. "Still. Can't bring myself to go back. I get all sweaty and can't breathe. And like I said, I can't anyway."

"What if I went back for you? I could find your dad."

The light above Harry's head flicked like there'd been a power outage somewhere. "Are you conning me, Harry Blunt?"

Harry shook his head. "No. If your father has been on Earth for…how long?"

"1,537 and a half years."

"Over 1,500 years. He'll have a history. Money. I'm an accountant. I follow money. I'll be able to find him. I know I will. I can help."

"You seem a little too eager."

"Of course I am. I help you. You help me."

"A deal?"

Harry nodded. "Sure. One of those."

Betuine sucked on a rib and looked Harry up and down, from his bare toes to his balding head. "You know how to make a deal?"

Harry put his hands in his pockets and tried not to hold his breath.

Betuine wiped her hands on her onesie, leaving a brown streak of sauce down her front. "Alright. I want an actual, physical address. Where he lives. And a photo as proof."

Harry nodded and tried to stand up a little taller and stronger than he felt. "I want to go back in a way that I can help Rainey."

Betuine pulled another rib out the foil and licked the BBQ sauce off it. The scent wafted through the tunnel, making Harry's mouth water. She nodded. "I want to know how he spends his time. I want to know what's keeping him there. I want to know why he left me."

Harry paused for a moment then nodded. "I want seven days."

"I can give you three."

"I have seven days in Port Harker before my sentence starts. I want to use it all for Rainey."

"If Rainey Blunt is dying in three days, you only need three."

Harry pressed his hands to his chest. "Fine. I'll take three."

Betuine grinned. "You're not very good at making deals." She turned and walked into the dark. "I'm going to let you borrow the body I used when I went to Life. It's a good one. Sturdy."

Harry paused then took a step into the dark. The bulb above him lit up, then the next, then the next, all the way to a cast iron door at the end of the tunnel. "Like a corpse body?"

Betuine opened the door. The hinges squealed. "No, you idiot. Like a suit. That's all a body is. A suit for the soul. You can borrow one of mine."

"The one that got drowned and burned?"

"Unbunch your pants. I made a new copy and upgraded the wardrobe."

The light above Harry's head flicked off, leaving him in darkness for all of three seconds, then a new light flicked on. Not one single bulb but a flood of lights that filled a room so big that it felt to Harry like it had its own special gravity.

Harry stepped inside. For further than his eyes could see, he saw rack upon rack and row upon row of perfectly organised stationery, cleaning materials, and office supplies. Each row was labelled. Every box was straight. The only thing out of place was the dust. Every item was coated in a thousand years of the stuff.

"Beautiful, isn't it?" Betuine whispered in Harry's ear.

"What's it all for?"

Betuine grabbed Harry by his dressing gown lapels and pulled him down so they were nose to nose. "Did you just ask a stupid question? Am I going to regret talking to you?"

Harry shook his head.

"I collect useful things, Harry. Useful things. You made coat hangers for a living. What was *that* for?"

She let Harry go with a little shove, then reached up and took a rubber stamp from the fourth shelf. She blew the loose dust off it and rubbed the more stubborn particles onto her onesie.

"Your wrist."

Harry held his wrist up. In the place where Charon had put the blue eel stamp, Betuine Harker replaced it instead with a green one of a goose with wings out wide.

"This will get you back. In three days, the body suit will go to ash, and you will return. With Grimmer, no less. And he's not going to be pleased because you should not, I repeat, not, be going back. But like you said, I'm the boss. I run things around here."

Harry stared at the shelves, the stamp on his wrist, and Betuine Harker. "Now what?"

"Now, you take my private elevator to Life, and you work things out. Fast. You made a deal with me, Harry.

If you think making one with the Legendary Devil is dangerous, please know that I carry 1,500 years of resentment in my heart. Don't let me down." Betuine put the rubber stamp back, reached into a box on the bottom shelf, and pulled out a small, orange drawstring bag. She handed it to Harry. "Everything you need is in that bag, including a phone."

Harry blinked.

"I keep up. And anyway, where do you think the idea for the silly devices came from? I'll call you; I'd rather you didn't try to call me. I might be busy. I won't wish you luck, Harry. That suggests you might not succeed. Your priority is our deal. Locate my father. Your child comes second. I hope you understand that."

Harry nodded, gripped the bag in both hands, and didn't even notice that Betuine was guiding him between the towering metal shelves, each one filled with everything from cling film to frames with random happy family pictures showing people what life could be like. He only realised he'd been holding his breath when they stopped in front of an elevator. The type that any slightly enlightened lift inspector would decommission simply because it had "Installed in 1741" engraved above the gate.

"Get dressed before the elevator lands," Betuine shouted as a wooden door creaked shut, trapping Harry inside. "And don't you dare break the one rule. No one must know or even guess that you're Harry Blunt. Not that anyone would believe you."

Harry was sure he heard Betuine laugh and say, "Fun, fun, fuuuun," until her voice faded and there was silence.

▼

Somewhere on the other side of Port Harker, sitting with his jacket off, his shirt unbuttoned at the neck, his shoes off, and his feet dangling in a cool, koi-filled pond, Grim felt a twinge at the back of his neck. It passed quickly enough, for which he was grateful. It had been a tough week, and the last thing he needed was to have to chase some idiot down who thought they could escape Port Harker, outrun the desert, or survive the geese.

He took a deep breath in, lay back on the deckchair, pulled an apple from the tree above him, and took a bite. A garden snake curled into a tight ball and fell asleep on his lap. "That's it, my sweet. Never worked out what all the fuss was about," he mumbled, wiping an errant dribble from his chin.

DAY 1:

BACK TO LIFE

Harry pressed himself into a corner of the lift and sat on a conveniently placed seat. Maybe it was sitting down but the need to pee intensified.

"Hold it," Harry muttered as the lift lurched left then right like a learner driver trying to decide whether to use their first solo trip to get a burger at the beach or a beer in town.

After a pause, the lift dropped so fast Harry levitated for a moment before colliding with the seat when the elevator jerked to a standstill, selected *Moon River* as the song of the day, and then, smooth as its five-star cousin, floated up.

Harry unclenched his hands from the railing. "This is madness! Maybe I'm dreaming." He stood still for a moment. "No. Too real." Forcing his fingers to work, he unknotted his dressing gown. "Get dressed, Harry."

The elevator swayed. Harry pressed his hand to his chest to slow his heart. "Breathe. One thing at a time." He let his gown fall to the floor and pulled his pyjamas off. Standing in nothing but underpants and bare feet, he paused and glanced at the door. "What if it opened right now? Where will it open? In the middle of the house? A street? A shopping centre? I didn't ask enough questions. Am I really going to see my kids?" Harry grinned and danced on one foot. "I did it! Did I? I think I did!"

He ripped the laundry bag open. Inside, he found a burgundy corduroy skirt with a matching jacket, a large, beige cotton shirt, a 36DD bra, beige tights, full-cover ladies' knickers, and black, flat slip-on shoes.

"What the…?" Harry shook the bag then peered inside. A brown, patent leather handbag, worn and scratched, was nestled in the bottom. He hauled it out and opened it to find a collection of stuff so random that it looked like Betuine was blindfolded when she packed it: a disc of original Vaseline lip balm, a small tube of hand cream for aging hands, a box of teabags, a teaspoon, a notebook and one…two…four pens, a large, black, rectangular purse, an extra pair of beige XXL tights, an empty plastic bag, a mobile phone that was first released the year Rainey was born, half a pack of chewing gum, a hairbrush matted with grey hair, a shiny Yale key alongside a larger, antique brass key, and a letter of employment from an agency stating that Harriet Sharp was the new lawyer standing in while Max Tiggis Snr. was on sick leave.

"Sick leave? What did you do to Max?" Harry shouted at the elevator ceiling but got nothing except the *Moon River* chorus on repeat.

Harry opened the purse. A photo of a round-faced, brown-eyed, curly-haired, slightly annoyed woman looked back at him. "Got that right," he muttered and flipped through the purse until he came to the driver's license, a donor card, and an identity badge: Harriet Sharp, 5'6'', blood type O neg., universal donor, home address in Cardiff?

"Kids say my Welsh accent sounds Indian." Harry cleared his throat and repeated himself using his best Welsh accent. "And they'd be right."

With the elevator starting to slow, he pulled out a makeup mirror and held it up to his face. Harriet Sharp, age 46, with short, curly, brown/grey hair, brown eyes and a surprised look, stared back at him.

Harry couldn't say whether it was gravity or shock but when the elevator stopped and the door opened into what looked and smelled like a disinfected public toilet, he pulled up the skirt, dropped the knickers, rushed for the urinal, looked down, and froze.

"Ahhh. Right. Okay. Didn't think… I didn't think…" He let his words trail away and forgot the urgency for a moment.

Then, simply because he felt it was the polite thing to do, he closed his eyes and crab-walked his way to the sit-down toilet, sat, and let nature and gravity take over, all the while refusing to look down.

"Oh, Lord, help me," Harry Blunt muttered as he straightened the skirt over Betuine Harker's all female form.

Still feeling the hot blush on his face but dressed as best as he could (tights in the bin), Harry cleared his throat. "Hello, I'm Harriet Sharp." His voice was high-pitched with a nervous edge. "Hello." He tried to lower the pitch. "I'm Harriet Sharp." He cleared his throat again. "Sounds like I'm 16 going on 60."

Standing at the door leading out of the public toilet, Harry tried to listen and guess where he was. He heard a breeze through the trees, someone talking, birds, and a car driving by. Harry grinned. Beyond the disinfectant, he smelled rain and autumn leaves, the splendid, mulchy scent that makes you think of firesides and cocoa.

With an image of Rainey fixed in his mind, he gripped the handbag with both hands and opened the door to Fairfig's town square on a wet, autumn morning exactly three weeks after he died, the day his will was to be read to his three, grieving children.

▼

"Home." Harry smiled, straightened the skirt with both hands, and, standing tall as Harriet Sharp could, stepped out of the public toilet and into a small park in the centre of Fairfig's town square.

The park consisted of a dozen trees, three picnic tables, paths between competition-level flowerbeds, and the toilet block. A young man wearing a black suit, white shirt, and no tie leaned against the railing outside the stone building smoking a cigarette. Harry knew him well. Arty Franks. Runs an estate agency in the square.

Harry glanced left then right. No one looked at him…her. "This is too much," he muttered and tried to stand in a way he thought a middle-aged woman would stand but didn't know what to do with his hands. He stuck them into the jacket pockets and leaned against the wall of the public convenience. A woman walked by with a child, smiled, then frowned and hurried on, holding the child close to her.

Harry took a breath in, let it out, found a bench, and sat.

"Right. I'm Harriet Sharp. I'm a lawyer. I'm a woman. I have three days to save Rainey's life. What the hell can I do in three days without anyone knowing who I am?"

Feeling the warmth of the sun on his face, Harry closed his eyes and leaned back. The birds sang, a breeze shuffled leaves around his feet, the smell of roast chicken and chips seeped out of the Two Beagles Inn across the square, and Arty Frank's voice cut through it all.

"Not a lot going on," he said to the person on the other end of the phone then bit into an egg mayonnaise sandwich, letting a dollop of filling drop into a barren rose bush beneath him. "Nah. The Blunt estate isn't going anywhere. Kids inherit everything. No surprise." He laughed at something the other person said. "Yeah, right. I tried to get my old man to make me his only heir to every damn thing, and he gutted his investments and bought a sodding vineyard in Spain just to make sure I get nothing." He bit into the sandwich again and tossed the remains into the shrubbery. Then, he laughed and kept talking, but Harry didn't hear any of it.

Kids inherit everything.

Harry hobbled from one bench to another just to get away from Arty Franks. He knew Arty's dad. Everyone thought the old man had gone mad when he'd remortgaged his house, sold his assets, including his interest in the real estate business, and bought a hundred acres in Spain to grow grapes.

Grateful to be wearing flat, sensible shoes, Harry sat on a low brick wall surrounding the park in the middle of the square. He dropped his head and blinked at his short, chipped, roughly painted pink nails. He buried his fingertips into his fists. "This is insane. Sending me back as a woman. Betuine Harker's having a proper laugh at all this." He stood up, paced in a circle, and sat back down again.

"You alright, Missus?" Arty Franks asked.

Harry looked at him and, for a moment, considered what the man was seeing: a dumpy, corduroy-clad, red-faced, middle-aged woman sweating slightly in the cold autumn air.

"Ahhhh…" Harry sat up straight. "Fine. Thank you. I'm fine. Just had some news. I'm fine."

Arty Franks wiped his hands on his trousers. "As long as you're fine then." The young man nodded and stood up straight. "Well, back to work for me." He ambled away, hands in his pockets, humming a tune Harry didn't recognise.

Harry waited until Arty Franks sauntered across the town square past two charity shops that used to be boutiques and a bookie that used to be a charity shop. He kept watching as Arty dodged around Blackfoot Bob, the local homeless man who refused every offer of shelter saying he liked to breathe at night, and ducked into the Two Beagles Inn.

With no one there to watch him, Harry finally stood up again, shifted from foot to foot to check his balance in this new body, and walked as straight as the new shape allowed toward the building that housed the office of *Max Tiggis: Family Law*.

Made of red sandstone with weathered monkey gargoyles on either side of oak double doors, Harry had met Max there every afternoon before they strolled to the local coffee shop to update each other on the worlds of family law and small business accounting.

Harry rifled through Betuine's handbag. "Damn handy thing this. Holds everything." He pulled out the two keys, one shiny and new and one as old as the building. "Thought of everything, Betuine. Very good of you."

He used the old, brass key on the wooden front door, the shiny Yale on the interior glass door, and stood in the middle of the plush but homely reception area of the only law firm in town.

Harry ran his hand along the magnolia paint that hid drawings Rainey had etched in the plaster while he and Max had talked about wills, and stocks, and shares. Harry had laughed when he saw the ink she'd left on the wall. Max hadn't found it that funny.

Harry glanced at the clock on the wall. 1:45 p.m. The kids would be here in a little over an hour. His kids. His boys and his beautiful baby girl. A rush of tingling joy flooded Harry's borrowed belly. He beamed. "I'm actually doing this! How is this even happening?" He tapped his feet, turned around twice, did a jig, arms waving and all, then caught himself in a hallway mirror. "Right," he muttered. "Play the part. Work to do."

He locked both front doors behind him and ducked into his old friend's office.

"Think, think, think!" Harry muttered. "Rainey has to wake up and live her own life. I can't just take her out of the will. Her brothers will put her back. Take them all out?"

Harry paced the office that looked like it had been decorated in 1803 and, except for an upgrade in phone technology and the reluctant addition of a computer, had been left unchanged.

"Arty Frank," Harry muttered. "Arty Frank owns that real estate business now. His old man made him buy him out or lose the agency." Harry opened the top drawer of an Edwardian letter filing cabinet. He rifled through the files until he came to the one he was looking for: *Last Will and Testament of Harry Samual Blunt.*

Using the old desktop computer Max had refused to change since IBM was all the rage, Harry logged into his account in *The Tiggis Legal Portal*. The online system had been a requirement forced on Max by, in his words, "kids who had no idea how the legal profession worked and how little interest we have in newfangled fads." Seeing all his legal documents in one place, Harry had to disagree.

He took off the jacket, pulled the skirt up around his waist, tossed the shoes into a corner, and loosened the buttons around his neck. Then, he laced his fingers and pulled them back until they clicked. "Right. Things are about to change for the Blunt family tree. Rainey needs problems. They all need problems."

Harry typed. "No... That's too much of a problem. Can't do that." He typed a little more. He deleted, added, replaced, and muttered. "Three days...hmmmm. Right. The cars..." Harry ummed, and ahhed, and mumbled as he typed and edited, rewrote and tweaked a will he'd spent three years creating. "Dates," he muttered. "Change the dates...got it...of sound mind..."

An hour later, banging on the door pulled Harry away from the screen. "Good enough." He printed the new document. "Signatures! Bother. Didn't think..." Harry glanced around the wide, mahogany desk. "Max won't mind." He picked up his friend's favourite pen, signed the will, then added a scrawl that could, unless examined, pass for the signature of Max Tiggis himself as a witness.

"I deserve to go to Hell," Harry muttered, then he logged out of the account, filed the new will, shredded the old one, strode out of Max's office, unlocked the front door, then promptly locked it again.

"Hello?" A voice said from the other side.

Harry closed his eyes. *Ben. My boy, Ben.*

Harry frowned and looked down: barefoot with the skirt around his hips and his shirt half-buttoned. "Oh, my Lord. Get it together, man." Harry straightened the skirt and buttoned the shirt. "How do women do it? Shoes." He ran back to Max's office, grabbed the jacket, slipped on the shoes, inspected himself in the hallway mirror, and was about to open the door when he heard all the voices he thought he'd never hear again.

"Everything okay?" Rainey said.

"Yep. I guess. Maybe the old guy's on the loo or something."

Harry smiled. Zach. Always a reason for everything.

Another knock on the door. "He said 3 p.m. Are we early?"

Ben. Double-checking everything.

Harry closed his eyes. "I'm Harriet Sharp. Lawyer. Standing in for Max Tiggis, who's on sick leave. Yes, he's alright. He'll be back in the office in a few days." Harry practised the line once more, stuck a smile on his new face then peeled it off because it didn't look right or appropriate for the circumstances, and unlocked the door.

"Hello," he said to the three perfect humans standing on the steps in front of him. "Excuse me."

Harry turned around, marched through the reception area, strode into the men's room, took one look at the urinals, strode back out again, and marched into the lady's room. He looked around him. One cubicle. Nowhere to hide. The door swung open and Rainey, his Rainey, his little girl, his beautiful baby, stood in front of him.

"Hello." She smiled. "I'm Rainey. Is Max not here?"

Harry cleared his throat and turned to the sink. He pumped half the container of soap into one hand and rubbed the mass over both hands. "Ahhhh. No. He's sick. I'm standing in." He tried to turn the tap on to rinse but, between the slime of the soap and how tight the tap was, did nothing except smear the lime-scented, antibacterial substance over every surface. "I'm Harr…Harri…Harriet Sharp. Colleague. I'm taking over for a while."

Rainey pulled paper towels from the box next to the sink and used them to grip and open the tap. Cool water washed over Harry's hands.

"I've done that so often," she said. "Have you known Max long?"

Harry kept his hands under the tap to give him something to do and a reason not to look at his child. *Don't cry. Don't. Cry!*

"Yes. Yes, I've known Max for thirty years. Old family friend."

"He's a good man. Can I ask…" Rainey paused.

Harry looked up in time to see a tear roll down Rainey's face. She wiped it away. "Sorry," she said. "It's been a difficult few weeks. Did you know my dad? He and Max go way back, too."

Harry almost dried his hands on his skirt when Rainey handed him another paper towel. "Yes," he said after a moment. "I knew your father."

Rainey pressed her lips together the way she always did when she had feelings, worries, and fears she didn't know how to express. Then, she smiled a tiny smile that vanished almost as fast as it appeared. "I miss him," she whispered.

Harry twisted and scrunched the paper towel between his hands until it shredded. Every fibre, cell, and particle in his body ached to hug her. "Is everything okay, Rainey? I mean. I know about your dad. But anything else?" Harry reached a hand out then pulled it back.

Rainey ignored Harry's hand, leaned in, and hugged.

For a moment, Harry didn't move. He just felt his daughter's arms squeeze. The smell from her skin and her hair. Coconut and apple. Her favourite scents since she was two years old. A sob escaped Rainey's lips. Harry hugged. "It's okay," he whispered. "I've got you. I've got this. You're going to be alright."

Rainey pulled back. "I'm so sorry. I'm sorry. It's just that things have been so strange. Things keep happening."

"Like what?"

"Stupid things. I nearly got hit by a car last week. I think I looked, but I probably didn't. Ben saved me." She dropped her face into her hands. "I was probably just distracted. Then, Zach had to go to hospital. He'd eaten something that must have gone bad."

"Is he alright?"

Rainey nodded. "He's fine. He's totally fine. Had his stomach pumped. Doctors don't know what it was. We had to clean out the whole fridge and throw everything away. Then, because Ben's paranoid, he emptied out the pantry too."

Rainey started to cry again. "He threw away the marmalade my dad made. He made the best marmalade, but Ben said he wouldn't take chances. 'What the hell?' I said to him." Rainey blinked at Harry with wet, wide eyes. "It feels like everything's falling apart. Everything. My dad..." Rainey pulled another paper towel from the box on the wall. "I'm sorry. Here we are. I've just met you, and I'm letting all the crazy out."

"It's okay. What about your dad?"

"He'd have fixed everything. He was like Santa." She wiped her face and smiled. "One day, things would be one way, and the next day, it'd all just be sorted."

"Christmas every day."

Rainey tilted her head and paused before she spoke. "That's what he used to say." She shook her head and folded her arms like she was barring entry to a thousand memories. "I'm sorry. I don't even know you. I shouldn't be talking this way. I just…" She sighed. "The boys are hard to talk to. They don't always listen."

"Brothers can be tricky, I suppose."

Rainey nodded and took a breath. "I miss my dad. I know, I've said that."

"He misses you too," Harry said, before he could stop himself.

Rainey smiled and wiped her face. "Thank you. I like to think so."

A knock on the door caused Rainey to turn around, giving Harry a moment to close his eyes and slap himself on the cheek.

"Everything okay in there?" Ben said.

Rainey turned back to Harry and squeezed his hand. "I'm glad you're here. I like Max, but I like you more."

Harry smiled. "Thank you."

"Rains?" Ben knocked again.

"Coming, Ben." She rolled her eyes and smiled. "They don't understand girl time."

Harry nodded. "I'll be with you in a minute."

The moment Rainey left the room, Harry ducked into the toilet cubicle, locked the door, and sat down. He wrapped his arms around his borrowed body and rocked. "Keep it together. Keep it together. Breathe, Harry. My name is Harriet Sharp. I'm standing in for Max Tiggis who's on sick leave. He'll be back in a few days. My name is Harriet Sharp. I'm a lawyer. I'm a professional."

Harry took one more breath then stood up, buttoned the jacket like armour, and went to meet his children for the first time since the day he died.

▼

In the 13th Circle of Hell, Betuine Harker paced the length of her bedroom. The window looked out over the River Cocytus. Unlike the gross misrepresentation by the infernal Dante, the Cocytus was a gleaming, streaming, deep blue river that started in Grimmer's garden, connected every circle of H.E.L.L., and ended in the lake that surrounded the Mink's Tail Tavern.

"Harry Blunt," Betuine muttered and paced. "A deal's a deal. He gonna find me my daddy." She punched her fists together. If a walnut had been caught between them, it would have shattered to dust. "And I'm going to crush him. Crush him!"

Betuine picked up a cushion she'd kicked around the room until it gave up and split a seam. She opened a window and let a cool breeze in. "He's going to pay, and pay, and pay." She leaned out the window and tossed the pillow out. Feathers escaped, leaving the cotton cover to settle on the surface of her favourite river. An eel curved and writhed, opened its mouth, swallowed the fabric whole, then spat it out. "That's gonna be you, Daddy. Swallowed and spat out. Over and over."

Betuine closed the window and pressed her head on the glass. "Harry Blunt will make that happen." She stood up straight and tucked a lock of hair under a paper crown she'd made just that morning. "I'm a number one priority to Harry Blunt. All I got to do is wait and be nice. Nice. Nice for Harry."

Betuine sat on the edge of her bed, laced her fingers together, and swung her feet backwards and forwards. "Harry will make it happen. Harry better make it happen."

THE WILL

Dressed in his signature, off-the-rack, tailored-to-fit, navy suit, Harry's oldest boy, Ben Blunt, stood at the door to the lawyer's office. Harry's hands gripped his own tweed jacket to stop him from wrapping his arms around his son. He'd inherited his serious face from Harry himself but his heart from his mother.

"Is Max going to be here today?"

Harry shook his head and stepped into the office. "No." He cleared his throat again. "Excuse me. Bit of a throat condition. All good. I'm fine. It's all…" He held out his hand. Ben took it and shook. Harry let go when he glimpsed his reflection in the glass of a picture frame. *Harriet Sharp. Harriet Sharp. Get with it.*

Harry cleared his throat one last time and accepted the higher-pitched tones of his borrowed body. "Mr. Tiggis is on sick leave. Nothing serious." He paused. "I'm sorry for your loss. Your father was a good man."

Harry looked from Ben to Zach, his middle child.

Neither boy said anything. They just nodded and sat; Ben on the chair in front of Max Tiggis' desk and Zach on the sofa that would have given him the best fireside spot if it had been lit.

"Our dad had been sick for a while," Zach finally said.

"Still." Harry pressed his hands together then became conscious, again, of the chipped nail polish on his fingertips.

"Are you alright, Ms. Sharp?" Rainey said. "You look a little pale."

Harry finally turned around and faced his daughter. "I'm fine, my…ahhh, Rainey. Rainey Victoria Blunt. Beautiful name."

Rainey smiled. "I'm named after my grandmother on my mother's side. My middle name is hers. I have no idea where my parents got my first name."

Harry smiled. He remembered. No, nothing as obvious as it being a rainy day on the day she was born. She got her name thanks to a priest who'd found his way from the hospice wing of the All Saints Hospital to the maternity ward. The old man was clearly lost and a little confused because he went from room to room showering women in labour with blessings to see them into the next life.

When he arrived in the Blunt family room, he'd started to run out of words to say. So, over and over, he waved his arms and bellowed, "Let all goodness reign and reign for evermore, reign like rain upon your heads, and may your vision for your life never be hemmed or reined in by evil, wickedness, or fear. Instead, let joy upon joy reign for as long as ye shall live. For peace be upon your soul, and the Lord…"

Harry chuckled at the memory. Jess, his beautiful wife and mother to his children, had been so stunned by the priest's ravings that she hadn't noticed Rainey had popped right out. The name seemed a natural fit after that.

"I'm sure it came from a beautiful place," Harry said when he noticed all three kids staring at him. He clapped his hands. "So, we're here to read the will, settle your father's estate, and help you move on with your lives. Do you have any questions before we begin?"

Ben took the lead. Harry expected no less. "No." He unbuttoned his jacket and leaned forward. "Please, go on."

The walk from one side of the desk to the other, where the new will sat in a brown folder, was the longest Harry had ever walked in his previous life.

He sat, pressed his hands on the document, and looked up at the expectant faces of his children. Ben sat patient and passive, never one to act without full knowledge of the facts. The family joke was that Ben could break both legs falling out a tree and not have an opinion on whether the break was real until he saw the X-rays for himself. Zach, on the other hand, would declare himself crippled for life and doomed to an early demise at the smallest hint of a simple sprain.

Jess… Harry paused for a moment. His wife, his lover, his best friend died too soon. Where is she now? She would chuckle every time she put a plaster on Zach's knee. "Just because you're an artist," she'd say and kiss him on the cheek, "doesn't mean you have to suffer."

But suffer Zach did. In the most comfortable fashion.

Rainey sat on the chair next to Ben. There was a time when she was always next to Ben, never more than a hand's reach from her big brother. Of course, as she got older, she began to turn to others, but Ben was always first. He rested a protective hand on her shoulder.

"Whenever you're ready," Ben said.

Harry opened the folder, then he paused and looked up at all three. His gut churned to the point of nausea.

He could pretend nothing had changed. He remembered his previous will word for word. Everything goes to the kids.

Ben gets the business in its entirety. Everything. People will always need coat hangers, and *Hangers By Blunt* made the best. Ben had pretty much run the business since Harry had fallen ill. He knew it inside and out. He had four business partners to rely on. All good people.

Zach was the artist he always wanted to be. The family business was his biggest, and actually his only, patron. One of Zach's sculptures stood in front of the factory; a three-story tall metal giant of what Zach said was a modern representation of the battle between man and nature. Harry wasn't sure he could see it, but Zach was so proud of it. So, there it stood. His next monolith was bronze and found a home in the family backyard by the duck pond. Harry could forget the changes he'd made in the last hour and announce that Zach's patronage would stand for life. An artist needs a patron. All artists need patrons!

And Rainey. Harry looked down at the brown folder. Rainey.

She could keep her trust fund. It would see her safe and supported for her entire life (Harry blinked a tear away), which would end in three days.

Harry took a breath, opened the folder, and read, "The Last Will and Testament of Harry Samual Blunt."

He looked up at his children one more time then didn't look up again until he'd read every word of the new and updated will.

He ignored the outrage, shock, and questions from Ben. He blocked out the sobs, wails, and gasps from Zach. He only listened to the silence from Rainey. She sat still through the entire reading. She didn't move. She didn't speak.

When the will was read, she turned to Ben. "What does it mean?" she asked.

Ben turned to his sister. "It means that Dad has completely hung us out to dry. This is insane. How can I not get the business? It's all I've ever done."

Harry closed the folder. "It's not that you don't get the business, Ben. It's that you get to decide whether the family business is what you want. If it is, then you can interview for the job. If you get it, then you can stay, but maybe you don't want to run the family business. Maybe you want to do something else. Maybe you want to start your own business?"

Ben stood up. "This is preposterous. Why would I want to start my own business when my name is already on the one my father built."

"I think that's the point," Harry said. "Your father built it. What do you want to build?"

Zach stood up. "I don't give two bollocks what Ben wants to build. I'm an artist. That's what I do. It's who

I am. There's no way my dad would cut me off. No way. Where's Rainey?"

For a moment, Ben and Zach stared at each other. Communication passed between them that Harry wasn't party to.

"That sneaky little bastard is not welcome here." Zach peered into the hallway as the front door slammed shut. He rolled his eyes. "And here he is. Like today couldn't get any sodding worse."

"Here who is?" Harry pulled the will towards him.

"Dusk Hamilton," Ben muttered. "Rainey's boyfriend."

Harry blinked. "Rainey has a boyfriend? When did that happen?"

Ben frowned. "He showed up when Dad got too sick to be out of bed. Goddamn gum on a shoe is all he is. He's doing the whole *I'll love and protect you forever* routine. For some insane reason, Rainey's falling for it. No idea what she sees in him."

Before Zach or Ben could say anything more, Rainey stepped back into the office holding hands with a young man dressed in a white, linen suit. Dark, thick hair was combed and groomed into an unnatural shape on his head and his brown eyes looked to Harry like mud pools. Was he wearing eyeliner? No. Couldn't be.

Harry stood up. "And you are?"

Dusk Hamilton didn't step forward, smile, or even blink. "Dusk Hamilton the Third. Rainey said there's a problem?"

"Nothing to do with you, Hamilton." Ben turned his back on the man. "This is family business."

"Then it has everything to do with me."

Zach, Ben, and Harry stared at Rainey and the newcomer. Not a word was spoken when Rainey lifted her hand to reveal a day-old engagement ring.

"No," Ben finally said.

Harry swallowed and sat. "The reading of the will is complete."

▼

Happy for any reason to drop into Life and Earth, Karma leaned against a tree outside the office of *Max Tiggis: Family Law*. What started out as a smile bloomed into a chuckle and finally a belly laugh that made her sit down on the manicured lawn.

"Harry, Harry, Harry Blunt. What in all things holy are you doing? So many questions." She took a small notebook from one pocket in her black leather jacket and a thin pencil from another. She flipped through her notes until she came to the Blunt family line, rubbed out a sentence or two, and watched the family through the window. Rainey Blunt gripped the hand of the boy next to her and blinked like the proverbial rabbit in headlights. Karma scribbled a few words in her notebook. "And so, the butterfly flaps her wings."

Relishing a bit of light afternoon entertainment, Karma lay back in the grass and watched the sun drift across the sky. The argument inside the lawyer's office grew so violent that people passing by stopped, stared, and walked on to spread the news that Harry Blunt had cut all his kids out of his will. More than that, he'd given them three days to turn the household contents into cash. After three days, everything left: the house, cars, other properties, artwork…would go to charity.

"You know, Harry was quite the collector." A woman wearing a leather hat and hiking boots paused outside the office in which Ben was doing all he could to stop Zach punching Dusk Hamilton in the face.

"Antiques," she said to her friend ever so casually glancing through the window. "Watches and clocks in particular."

The friend craned her neck, stood on her toes, and peered through the glass just in time to see Dusk Hamilton punch Zach in the belly, knocking the man backwards and causing Ben to lunge forward and defend his brother, getting him kicked in the head for his troubles. Rainey covered her face and ran outside, and the lawyer stood behind a six-foot yucca plant doing nothing at all.

"Got grandfather clocks in his house that London museums are interested in," the woman muttered. "And sculptures."

"Ohhh, not the silly stuff the Zach boy creates. Didn't I hear Harry had a Rodin?"

"I heard he had two."

"I heard the Hamilton boy is after it all."

"Did he and Rainey honestly get engaged yesterday?"

"You'd think she could do better."

Karma breathed in a lungful of delicious human air, closed her eyes, and soaked in the sun. Harry Blunt had been clear. She wouldn't have believed it if she hadn't heard it herself. Everything not sold in three days would go to charity. Zach Blunt's patronage had three months left to run and then would cease. Ben Blunt had been fired from the family business effective immediately and must apply for his job if he really wanted it. Rainey Blunt's trust fund would cease to be in three days. And then there's Dusk Hamilton.

"Bloody brilliant," Karma chuckled then ambled into Fairfig town to see what other trouble the humans who lived there were getting themselves into.

SNOOPING AROUND

It was well after dark before Harry finally got rid of Zach and Ben. Dusk Hamilton had chased after Rainey as soon as he was sure the brothers understood he was more willing to draw blood than they were.

"Oh, my holy bloody hell in a handbasket," Harry said, not for the first time. The words that finally got the boys out the office were that the auctioneers would be at the family home at 7 a.m. on Monday morning.

Harry bolted the doors shut then went to every room to check the windows and close the curtains. Not that he thought his children would do anything violent or unexpected, like break into the office. It wasn't them he was worried about. It was Dusk Hamilton. He was the one who made Harry's borrowed body feel like ants had taken residence under his skin. How had he missed it? What possessed his daughter to want to marry someone like him? If he married her for money, he'll be disappointed.

Satisfied the building was secure, Harry went back to his friend's office and switched on the computer. *Dusk Hamilton Fairfig* he typed.

Pictures of the young man sprang up, mostly of him with friends. A few were with a brother and two sisters. Another was with his parents at a graduation event. The rest were of Dusk Hamilton himself; drinking, dancing, sticking his tongue out at the camera (his favourite pose), doing idiot things with his brother, Grayson Hamilton, who is younger by two years and two days, and worst of all, with his Rainey. Everywhere.

"How had I missed this? She never mentioned him. Never brought him home."

Harry glanced at a photo of his old friend, Max Tiggis. "It's not that she didn't talk about him to me. Maybe she did, and I just didn't hear her through the drugs. There's something about him, Max. Something wrong and broken."

Harry dug through Dusk Hamilton's social media images and stopped when he came to a selfie of the lad over Harry's freshly dug grave. Rainey and the boys were in the background, hugging each other, walking towards the cars. Hamilton was striking his usual pose over the open grave. The picture showed Harry's coffin, soil-covered in fake green grass, and two men leaning against a digger. Hamilton himself was grinning into the camera with his tongue out. He had two fingers up and "blingbling" as a caption.

Harry rubbed his eyes. "What have I done?" He took a breath and was just about to close the computer when he paused. "Betuine Harker. Right." He tapped the keyboard and typed another name: Jack Harker.

Google didn't disappoint. Or maybe it did. Pages of images, news reports, and social links, all leading to various versions of Jack Harker, filled his screen: engineers, skateboarders, some bodybuilding type next to a high school kid, an author, a proud dad, a retired soldier. It was a constellation of Jack Harkers.

Harry tapped the mouse light enough to keep it awake but not do anything. "Got to be a way to narrow this down." He clicked a button here and another one there. Harry nudged and stretched the bra he wished he'd thrown out along with the tights. Women were clearly not consulted in the design of their underwear. He was just about to quit when he clicked a small arrow with "Filter" next to it and saw his favourite word: finances.

"Follow the money." He adjusted the filter.

Businesses. Harry pressed his lips together. He started to dig. "If I was a 60,000-year-old man who'd lived on earth for the last 1,500 years, what would I do with my time?" Harry flicked through images and numbers, statistics and news articles. "If I had all the time in the world and didn't want to be found, didn't want to stand out but also wanted to be comfortable, what would I do? Money, money." Harry opened a website only he and people in his particular field of accounting had access to. "Generational wealth," Harry murmured. "Not a lot you can hide when human nature takes over."

Harry tried to smile. His face ached. The muscles felt unused. "I suppose Betuine never had much to smile about. And her dad," Harry stared at the computer screen, "was the reason for her misery." He stabbed the keyboard harder than he should. "Bad fathers should be hung out to dry."

Harry frowned at the cursor and typed Jack Harker's name again.

Only one match came close to what Harry was looking for. Not even a full name. Just J. Harker. His business interests were registered with Generational Wealth Management back when the organisation was founded in 1844, which means they were older than that. Harry started to dig.

His search led him from Generational Wealth Tracker, to Company's House, to HMRC, to tax havens you had to know about to know they existed.

"Has to be," Harry finally muttered when he settled on a company name as bland and invisible as you'd expect a stationery maker to be: "JH Ink, purveyors in fine stationery since 1472." Harry used every financial and company tracker he had access to but found nothing except a small reference to a writing implement called the Harker Scribe in 687 AD.

JH Ink had offices in London and New York and provided stationery across the board, from mass market supermarkets to handcrafted collectibles.

"This could be anything and anyone. Could be a normal family business." Harry tapped a fingernail against the keyboard. "No photos of the owner." Harry frowned. "No stories about who owns it. No partners. No directors. Just one name." Harry clicked through a link that promised *more*... "And multiple businesses under one umbrella. JH Artisans, JH Legal Services, JH Guild of Engineers, JH Storage, JH Transport, JH Associates, JH Antiques."

Harry rubbed his chin then stopped when he felt soft skin instead of the stubble that usually grew out by the end of the day.

Most of the businesses opened and closed within a few decades. Some lasted over a hundred years. It was the umbrella company that held Harry's attention. He glanced back at his friend's framed photo. "Look at those numbers, Max. Look at those numbers and tell me you don't see what I see. Good heavens above. Our profits dipped within a month of Ben taking over full-time. Generational businesses don't just grow and grow. Children aren't that reliable or stable. Money ebbs, Max. It flows. It doesn't just keep on growing when new generations get their hands on it."

Harry looked back through the numbers and smiled. "Has to be him. Now I just need a home address and my deal with Betuine Harker is done, and I can focus on the Dusk problem."

Harry took a breath, and for the first time since the day he died, he felt he had things under control. "Might even get a little dinner on the way to seeing how the kids are getting on."

▼

Jack Harker leaned over what he called a desk, and others might, if they were being generous, call a workbench. In reality, it was a slab of wood resting on two stacks of breezeblocks. The desk, as Jack called it, had two 40" screens, a Quinair Tenth Gen Supercomputer hand built for him by a kid in Mumbai, a stack of Post-it notes, and a chipped coffee mug holding an assortment of pens, including the prototype of the original Harker Scribe, identifiable only by a tiny goose engraved near the nib and its unparalleled quality.

He tapped the keyboard and followed the search that someone, somewhere on the planet, was doing on him. It took less than three minutes for Jack Harker to have the IP address for one Max Tiggis, Family Attorney, Fairfig, England.

"What does Max Tiggis want to do with me?"

Jack opened a piece of software that the kid who built his computer added for a small fee, tickets to the Grand Ole Opry for life. The software hacked into CCTV systems anywhere in the world.

"You don't get to live as long as I do, Max Tiggis, without being a little bit nosey."

Jack Harker typed in the street address linked to the IP address, and a dim evening street filled the screen. Nothing happened for a while, so he used the time to call his pilot and schedule a flight from London to Farringdon Farm airfield. It wasn't so much an airfield but a long lane on a piece of land he'd won off an oil tycoon a hundred and eighty years earlier.

Door to door, considering it was a Tuesday night and London traffic shouldn't be an issue, Jack Harker calculated he'd be in Fairfig by just after midnight. He picked up a small overnight bag he always kept packed with a compass, a torch, matches, candles, three changes of clothes, a tin cup, teabags, a portable stove - normal things - and was just about to shut his computer down when the front door of Max Tiggis, Family Lawyer, opened.

Jack stared at the screen. He knew the body well. He just hadn't seen it in a thousand years. "Betuine?"

Jack Harker used every shortcut through London he had at his disposal, told his pilot to put his foot down, landed on the farm runway without the use of telltale lights, picked up a car he kept at the airfield in case of emergencies, and arrived in Fairfig's town square just before the church bell chimed midnight.

In the park in the middle of the town square, he sat on a bench and opened his laptop again. Once more, he hacked into Max Tiggis' computer and scoured the files and folders for recent work.

"The Last Will and Testament of Harry Samual Blunt," he read. He opened the document and saw the recent changes. "Betuine, my sweet, wicked child. What are you doing messing with this poor man's will?"

Jack Harker scrolled to the front page of the will and stopped when he came to the Blunt home address. He glanced at his watch and shrugged. "Just a little look around," he said as he climbed into the silver Ford hatchback he purchased with the intention of blending in and followed a map from where he was to the place where Harry Blunt had died just a few weeks prior.

BATTLE OF THE WILLS

Harry could have made the trip home in the dark, blindfolded, and tipsy. Two out of three wasn't bad. He wasn't blindfolded. A nip of whiskey with a light supper (chicken pie, chips, dessert, hold the veg) didn't sit well with Betuine Harker's body-on-loan. The moment he swallowed the 20-year-old malt, his head spun enough to keep him sitting quietly by the fire for an hour at least.

"You want anything else, Missus?" the owner of the Two Beagles Inn and a man Harry had known for thirty years asked.

Harry smiled and shook his head. "I'm fine, Jonesy. Just killing a little time."

Jonesy smiled like he always did no matter what his guests said. "Take all the time you need. We close at midnight."

Midnight. Harry frowned. Does this body need to sleep? "Ahhh, Jonesy? Do you have a room for the night? The next three nights actually."

Jonesy looked down at the beagle at Harry's feet. "Seems he's taken a liking to you."

"He's a smart dog."

"Knows an easy touch for treats when he sees one."

"The room?"

Jonesy nodded. "Sure. Room three's available. I'll put your dinner on your tab. Pick up the key at the bar."

Harry tried to get up, but the room swayed again. "This body can't handle alcohol. Should have guessed." Harry scratched Bernie the beagle behind the ear as Jonesy wove his way between tables, clearing glasses as he went. "You see me, don't you boy?" The dog licked Harry's hand, passed gas, and fell asleep.

Harry stared at the fire right up until the last bell rang when Jonesy announced closing time.

"Pretty sure the kids will have got things going. Time to check in." Testing his feet one at a time, Harry stood. The room didn't spin, but his gut roiled.

"Are you alright, Ms. Sharp?" Jonesy held the door open for guests as they left.

"Just need a little fresh air."

With his room key in hand, Harry stood on the pavement outside the inn. Autumn was coming. No real signs yet. Just a change in the air.

"If I can walk a straight line from here to Max's car, then I'm sober enough to check in with the kids."

"Are you sure you're alright, Ms. Sharp?"

Harry waved his hand. "Fine. Fine. See you in the morning."

"Your room is this way."

Harry waved again. "Just going to check on my clients. Just a quick visit."

Harry was already climbing into Max Tiggis' Bently when Jonesy reminded him it had gone midnight.

"They'll be up and about," Harry said.

And they were.

By the time Harry got to the house, he'd sobered up enough to recognise a riot when he saw one.

"Get the hell off my property, Hamilton. You scheming little shit-bag. I don't know how you got under Rainey's skin, but you're not welcome here."

"It's not just your property, Zach." Rainey ran out of the house and put her arm around Dusk Hamilton. "He's my fiancé. He has to be welcome here."

"He's not, Rains. I can't believe you can't see through him."

Dusk Hamilton shrugged Rainey off and took a step closer to Zach. Both men did what young men do: their chests puffed and their arms stretched out. Given a few billion years, Harry thought, these two probably met each other on the plains of Africa and had the same argument.

"You're one to talk. See through me? You're a fraud, Zach Blunt. Call yourself an artist? Other than your dad, name one other person who's bought your art. Just one. You've leached off your family your whole life. You think those statues are worth any damn thing? It was just your daddy paying for a glorified hobby. Not a particularly talented one at that. Who's going to pay you now? Three months and no more patronage?" Dusk Hamilton threw his head back and laughed.

Zach took a step forward. "You moron. Have you worked out yet that the tit you're sucking on is running dry in three days? Three days and Rainey has no more trust fund. Zip. Zero. Nada. Then what?"

Dusk Hamilton grinned then pulled Rainey to him and kissed her.

"Get your hands off my sister!" Ben bellowed from the front door.

"My fiancé!" Hamilton shouted back.

"She's ours, you piece of shit."

Zach launched himself at Hamilton. He got there just before Ben. Two against one and it still wasn't fair. The closest Zach and Ben had ever got to a physical fight were the occasional brotherly scraps. Dusk Hamilton had been born and raised playing dirty.

While the three men grunted, swore, and swung, Rainey covered her face and eventually ran inside and slammed the door shut.

Hiding behind a tree, Harry watched. "Leave them be," he whispered to himself. "You have to let them deal with this. It's their lives, their problem to solve. It's why you're here. Let it go. Stay where you are. Don't interfere. Don't. Interfere."

"You'll get nothing." Ben spat at Hamilton when he finally came up for air.

"That's where you're wrong." Dusk Hamilton wiped blood from a lucky punch off his face.

"Is there a problem here, gentlemen?"

Harry had been so focused on the fight that he hadn't noticed a car pull up next to Dusk Hamilton's motorbike. Big enough to be comfortable. Small enough to go unnoticed in any suburb.

The pictures Harry had found online were old, but the face hadn't changed.

"Jack Harker?" Harry said louder than he intended, covered his mouth with both hands to catch the sound, and hid behind the tree.

Dusk Hamilton scrambled to his feet. "None of your business. You can sod off and all." He tried to shove Jack Harker aside so he could get to Ben but found himself sprawled on the grass for his efforts.

"And you are?" Jack Harker held his hand out to Ben.

Ben shook hands out of habit and manners. "Ahhh, Ben Blunt. Do I…" Ben straightened his tie. "Do I know you?"

Jack Harker smiled. "No. We have a mutual acquaintance. Perhaps we could talk inside?"

One look from Jack Harker and Hamilton got back up again, swore, dusted grass off his jacket, and skidded away on his motorbike.

Harry had no choice but to watch Jack Harker, the first mayor of Port Harker, Betuine Harker's 60,000-year-old father, looking no older than a well-trimmed 45, disappear inside.

Ten minutes later, he reappeared, climbed into his car with the smallest glance Harry's way, and drove off in the same direction Dusk Hamilton had taken.

Harry stepped out from behind the tree, stood in the middle of the road, and had only one question: "What is Jack Harker doing here?" Truth be told, Harry had a whole lot more than one question: How had Jack Harker found his kids? What did he want with them? Did he know about the deal Betuine had made? Was Betuine playing some sick game with him? Was Jack Harker dangerous? What the hell just happened?!

Straightening the tweed jacket and raising the skirt so he could move with speed, he ran up the path and knocked on the door of the house he used to own, maintain, and live in.

Rainey answered. "What are you doing here? It's gone midnight."

Harry nodded. "Can I come in? I need to talk to you about the man who was just here."

Harry sidestepped Rainey and barged into the house. He didn't have to look left or right to know that the kitchen was at the end of the hall. "Where are your brothers?"

Just then, Ben stepped out of what had once been Harry's office. "Excuse me? Ms. Sharp? Do you need something?"

Harry turned to his oldest son. "What did that man want? Who did he say he was?"

"Funny you should ask. Turns out he's a lawyer, and he was asking all about you."

"You look pale, Ms. Sharp. Can I get you a cup of something?" Zach drained a mug containing a liquid Harry suspected would ignite if he lit a match.

Ben smiled. "Turns out the will isn't valid, and it can all go back to what it was. I still own and run the business which means Zach's patronage is safe and Rainey's inheritance is secure and in trust. That means that if Hamilton tries to steal anything, I, as the keeper of that trust, can sue the little shit."

Harry wondered for a moment why Ben's voice had dropped to a whisper and a wink until he glanced behind him to see Rainey almost sobbing into her phone. Harry focused on Ben. "Did he have proof of who he was? Identification?"

Ben tapped his fingers against the doorframe. Something he'd done since he was a child every time he needed to think before he answered. "He has about as much proof as you, Ms. Sharp. His bar exam results weren't tattooed onto his forehead, but he said enough of the right words for me to determine that yes, he was who he said he was."

Zach ripped open a bag of crisps and stuffed a handful into his mouth.

Ben kept talking. "We told Mr. Harker everything. He said he'd be able to reverse the change and give us our inheritance back. What do you say to that, Ms. Sharp?"

Harry blinked. "Did he leave a card? Contact details?"

Ben nodded. "Yes, but since you no longer represent the family, I don't see how it's your business. It's late. I'm going to ask you to leave. Max Tiggis and whoever's associated with that firm no longer represents the Blunt family. Thank you for your time."

"Oh, good Lord." Harry rubbed his face with both hands, but by the time he found any words, he was on the front porch, the door had been slammed shut, and the lights had all been put out.

"That's not good," he muttered. "This isn't good at all." Harry raised his hand to ring the bell, then stopped.

"Think, Harry. Think. Where would someone like Jack Harker go after picking up a new client in a new town at this time of night?"

Harry thought for a full minute and conceded that he had no idea, so he got back into Max's car, shoved it into gear, and drove back to the inn. The sign outside had been amended. A "Full" banner had been added.

"Right," Harry muttered and stared up at the dark windows above the inn. A breeze caused autumn leaves to drift from the tree above him onto the road. Harry only noticed he'd been standing in front of the inn longer than he intended when Bernie the beagle ambled out, had a long pee against a tree, then trotted up and sat at Harry's feet. Harry leaned down and scratched the animal on the head.

"I need to know more about Jack Harker," Harry said, then he pulled out his key and stalked into the side door of the Two Beagles Inn.

▼

Jack Harker watched Harriet Sharp from his darkened room above the inn. The room was small but clean. Just how he liked it. He liked a lot about Life on Earth. It had taken him around 1,000 years to get used to it, and he wasn't ready to leave yet. His daughter had tried to find him once before, and now she sends some silly sap in her body? To do what?

Jack Harker knew he had choices. You don't survive unscathed for this long without learning a thing or two about people and cunning plans.

Way he saw it, Jack had three choices. He could confront Harriet Sharp and demand she tell him what his daughter wanted and why she sent some lost soul in her body. He could strike up a casual conversation and subtly find out how and why Harriet Sharp was using one of his daughter's suits. Or he could snoop around until he found what he wanted without having to talk to the interloper at all.

Jack Harker weighed up the different approaches and realised he had a fourth option. He could leave the country until Betuine got bored of whatever game she was playing. Bolini Isle was nice this time of year. A little foggy, but there'd be room at his favourite inn for sure. Or maybe Iceland. Or Sakhalin. Hawaii…

Jack Harker closed his eyes and let the cool evening air settle around him. He only moved when Harriet Sharp pulled a key out of her bag and walked into the side door of the inn. He listened as a door leading to the first floor swung open and banged against the wall, causing the woman to swear.

For a moment, there was silence. Jack pressed his ear against his door and listened. If it wasn't for the age of the building, he was sure he wouldn't have been able to map Harriet Sharp's movements, but every step was another creak like the building had had enough of being walked all over and was finally objecting.

The creaking paused every dozen steps or so. It stopped in front of Room #4, the room Jack Harker had booked just an hour earlier.

Jack leaned against the door and listened. Did he hear breathing? He smiled.

"I guess I'm going to snoop around until I know what's going on," he whispered, and he couldn't stop the smile spreading across his face. "Got to love humans."

DAY 2:

WHEN HARRY MEETS JACK

The next morning (if you could call it that), Harry got up earlier than he ever did when he was alive. Truthfully, he hadn't slept at all. The whole "sleep when you're dead" notion just didn't seem funny now that he'd seen what happens next.

Not that he hadn't tried. He'd spent the first hour trying to sleep, then gave up and paced his room, waiting for the sun. When that took too long, he'd dialled Rainey a dozen times and hung up before the phone rang every time. Finally, at just past 3 a.m., he put the tweed jacket and skirt back on. A little dusty. A little sweaty, but good enough for what he had to do.

"Dusk Hamilton," he mumbled as he straightened the bed out of habit.

Harry might not be able to do much about Jack Harker, but he sure as hell could find out more about Dusk Hamilton. Glancing around his room, Harry stuck his room key into Betuine Harker's handbag.

Damn handy thing, this. He clipped it closed.

Dusk Hamilton's home address had been easy to find on social media. He shared every room in his house, every view of his street, and, ultimately, his actual address when he invited his friends and followers to his engagement party. Harry noticed it was "his" and not "their" engagement party. Had Rainey noticed? He wondered how that made her feel.

The drive over didn't take long since the most cautious driver can travel the breadth of Fairfig in less than an hour. Sticking to side streets, Harry arrived at the Hamilton family home a little after 3:30 a.m. and parked Max's Bentley a few doors down from the two-floor, detached house that was surrounded by a garden big enough to keep a small herd of cows.

The front gate was open, and Harry paused only once before sneaking inside. Staying close to the fence, he slunk around the edge of the property.

"I don't think they have CCTV," a voice said behind him. "Might have motion sensors."

Harry stood up and turned around, both fists raised high.

"Relax, Ms. Sharp. It's only me."

"Jack Harker. Jack sodding Harker. What the flying duck are you doing here? How did… What do you want?" Harry faced Betuine Harker's father square on. "How did you find me and get here so fast?" Harry paused. "I mean, who are you and what do you want?"

Jack Harker took a step back and frowned. "You're not very good at this, are you." It wasn't a question. "And you're not a woman in that body."

Harry straightened Betuine's jacket and stood up as tall and feminine as he knew how. "I don't know what you're talking about."

Jack Harker laughed. It was too loud and too long for pre-dawn illegal activity.

"Keep it down," Harry whispered. "You have no idea what you're walking into. You'll ruin everything. More than you have already."

"Me? Ruin things? If you knew what you were doing, maybe I wouldn't have to step in."

"Step into what?"

"Fixing the absolute mess you're about to make."

"You have no idea what's going on or what's at stake!"

"Then why don't you tell me?"

Harry didn't move or say a word.

Finally, Jack Harker shook his head. "Look. I don't want to mess anything up. I'm here because you're not particularly good at snooping. You left a trail at least a mile wide. All I know is someone is using my daughter's bodysuit, and that always ends up causing me problems I'd prefer to avoid. So, tell me what's going on, and maybe you and I can make a deal, and this can all end politely."

Jack Harker held his hand out as if the deal had already been agreed. "We can start with who you are."

Harry wasn't sure why, but he found himself shaking Jack Harker's hand. "Harry Blunt."

Jack Harker nodded like he approved.

Harry paused and frowned at the man for a moment. "Do you mind if we focus on the task at hand first? It's a little time sensitive."

Jack Harker leaned against the fence, took out a cigarette, and was just about to light it.

"Alright." Harry made to take the cigarette then stopped when Jack Harker's eyes turned sharp and a little hard. "I died, alright? Your daughter loaned me this suit so I could come fix a mess I left behind, which, by the way, you're not making any easier by undoing everything I've done. You cannot change my will. I took all my kids out of it for good reason."

"And?"

"And nothing."

"Your sob story aside, my daughter never does anything for nothing, and she never gives people free rides back to Life, especially not in her personally designed bodysuit. What deal did she make with you?"

Harry shook his head. Jack Harker lit his cigarette. The flame and glowing ember lit up his face and the tree behind him. Harry knocked it out.

"She wants to find you, alright? So, thank you for making that easy."

"She wants to find me. And?"

"Nothing. She wants your home address."

"Nothing else?"

"That's it! She wants to know where you are and why you deserted her. Nice going, by the way. Now, as great as it is to meet you, my priority at the moment is my own child. If you could leave details of where you live and how Betuine can contact you, we can talk later. Right now, I would very much like to find out what the hell Dusk Hamilton has in mind for my daughter."

Jack leaned forward and studied Dusk Hamilton's house. "Why do you think he has anything in mind?"

Harry squeezed his hands together then put them in his pockets. "Call it father's intuition. That boy's not right."

"House is dark. What do you think you're going to achieve here?"

Harry leaned against a tree. "I have no idea. I have two days left and no idea what the hell I'm doing. She's going to die before tomorrow is done. I know my boys won't hurt her, so unless it's a random accident…"

Jack Harker nodded. "Very likely."

"…then this boy… What do you mean *very likely*?"

"Have you met Karma?"

"She's here? You think Karma's going to…"

Jack held up his hand. "Look."

Harry turned towards the house. Dusk Hamilton ambled out of a side door, crossed over a cobbled driveway, went into a garage, and turned the light on. A moment later, his younger brother Grayson joined him. He had the same dark hair styled into unnatural shapes with mud-brown pools for eyes. Other than a small difference in height, the boys could be twins.

Harry and Jack melted into the trees when a van drove up the driveway and parked in front of the garage. Two men who looked like they were on day release from Wakefield Prison (tattooed, muscled, and open to drowning kittens for cash) got out and went into the space big enough to house four Hummers, closing the door behind them.

Harry ducked low, only because he'd seen folk do it in the movies, ran up the drive, and pressed himself against the wall of the garage under a window.

Jack Harker ambled up the drive and peered through the glass.

"What do you see?"

"The two big guys are just standing there. Hamilton the younger is opening a bottle of vodka, and Hamilton the elder is setting up for a game of pool."

"Pool?"

Jack mimed the shooting of a ball with a cue stick.

"I know what pool is." Harry stretched up and peered through the window.

The men talked about the game for a bit then about some sporting event Harry had never heard of. Finally, Grayson Hamilton got to the point. "You got a plan? One that'll actually work this time?"

"Are you kidding me right now? I set her up perfectly last week. Flowers and fricken teddy bears on one side of the road. She was completely distracted. All you had to do was drive. But no. You missed her."

"Her brother was there."

"So, you could have hit him too! Got them both out of the way."

Harry didn't move. His belly rolled over and he swallowed bile that rose up uninvited. He gripped the windowsill.

"Steady," Jack Harker whispered. "Take it easy."

Harry felt a firm, warm hand on his shoulder, and he breathed. "The little shit has been trying to kill my baby for weeks."

"Nothing you can do now except watch and learn."

Harry glanced up at Jack and turned his attention back to the boys in the garage.

Dusk shot a ball into a corner pocket. "I'll take Rainey out tomorrow night."

"Take out?"

Dusk Hamilton shot another ball and missed. "Some place fancy. Flash some cash. Then, take a shortcut through the park."

Grayson Hamilton chuckled. "Then what?"

Dusk glared at his brother. "Then you stay away. I don't want any Hamilton near anything associated with the Blunt family. It's what these boys are here for."

The two men crossed arms over barrel chests as a symbol of the pride they took in their work.

Dusk was still talking. "You boys jump us in the middle of the park. The bit by the stairs where the lights are out. I'll do the whole panic and cry thing." He raised the pitch of his voice and shot another ball in the back right pocket. "She's not breathing… I don't know what to do. I don't know what happened… We were attacked. Help!" The ball disappeared in the hole. He turned to the two men. "I'll call you from the hospital. Do nothing until you get word from me. Got it?"

The men nodded.

Hamilton lined up his cue again. "Soon as the brothers are at the hospital, I'll let you know that the house is clear, and you boys can get to work. You'll have at least a few hours. Hopefully, the whole night. I'll let you know if they head home."

"You expect her to survive?"

Dusk glanced at his brother. "I don't want her dead. What do you think I am? She's just the distraction." He stood aside while Grayson took a turn.

Grayson hit a ball and missed the pocket. "You sure this will work?"

"If everyone does their part, there's no reason it won't. I got photos of everything today. Got buyers lined up already."

Grayson and the two men took a step back and let Dusk take another turn at the table.

Harry turned his back on the game, leaned against the garage wall, and slid down until he sat. "Tonight? Oh, my God. He's going to kill Rainey. Tonight? I thought I had another day to make a plan."

Jack Harker settled beside Harry. "He just said he had no intention of seeing her dead."

"That's what he said, but you know what's going to happen."

"Isn't the whole idea to let them get on with things on their own?"

Harry shook his head. "They have to learn to clean up their own messes, not mine. I'm here to fix what I broke."

Jack closed his eyes for a moment. "Your kids will be broken no matter what you do. It's human nature."

"Says the parent of the sodding past twenty centuries."

Jack smiled. "Betuine was going to end up a little crazy no matter what I did."

"You deserted her."

"No, I left her in charge of her life on her own. There's a difference."

"You were supposed to run Port Harker."

Jack shook his head. "No. I just got roped in. What else was Betuine going to do with her time? Return to Life over and over and live on beaches? No. She had more to give and certainly more to learn."

"So, you gave her Port Harker so she had something to do?"

"I gave her Port Harker so she had problems to solve, and here she is solving them. Sending you to find me. And I don't plan on making it easy for her."

Harry shook his head. "I can't do it. If Rainey was just going to die and then get another Life, that's one thing, but that's not going to happen. This is it for her. If she dies, she's heading to the TV room. I can't let Hamilton be the one to do this."

Jack Harker let out a long, slow "Ohhhhhhhh." Then, he patted Harry on the shoulder. "Dusk Hamilton isn't responsible for Rainey ending up in the TV room. He's just the vehicle they're using to recall her."

"Murder is murder, and I won't let it happen."

"If they want her back, they'll find another way. I asked once, and I'll ask again. Have you met Karma?"

Harry ignored him. "There has to be a way."

Jack got up and ambled down the driveway, lighting another cigarette. "I'm sure you'll find it, Harry Blunt."

Harry stood. "Where are you going?"

Jack Harker didn't look back. "I have Life to live."

"Where exactly do you live?"

Jack pulled a small card out of his pocket, put it on the garden wall, and placed a rock on top of it. "Tell my daughter I say she's welcome to drop in anytime."

Harry watched the man disappear into the dark. Betuine Harker, at the very least, would get what she wanted.

▼

Karma sat on the double bed booked and paid for by Harry Blunt aka Harriet Sharp. She ran her hand over the blanket folded at the bottom of the bed then opened her notebook. With a pencil poised, she closed her eyes and felt for the tug of fortune's web.

"Consequence," she whispered as she scribbled a few lines on the page, tore it out, and put the paper on Harry's pillow. "Cause and effect," she said as she left Harry's room, meandered down the hall, pausing at Jack Harker's door for just the slightest of moments, and left the Two Beagles Inn so undisturbed that not even Bernie the Beagle dozing by the fire noticed.

THE WORST DAY OF HARRY'S LIFE (AND AFTERLIFE) SO FAR

5:07 a.m.

Harry's children slept. He knew this because he'd been sitting in the garden shed watching their house since Jack Harker had left him an hour earlier. The shed was the size of a single garage and was filled with half-empty pots of paint, garden tools, deckchairs, and a jungle gym the kids had loved when they were little that Harry had kept in the hopes of rebuilding it when grandkids came along.

No grandkids.

Harry sat on a wooden bench and stared out the window.

Why no grandkids?

Rainey was too busy focusing on being young. Zach was too focused on his art. Ben was too focused on the family business.

Harry stared at the clock on the wall.

"I can't sit here like this and do nothing!"

He sat there like that and did nothing for a minute more. He waited until it felt like shed spiders had taken up residence under his skin.

"I have to do something."

Harry left the shed.

5:09 a.m.

He straightened his tweed jacket and skirt as best he could, licked his thumb and rubbed mud off his shoes, and sniffed his armpit. Not pretty, but it'll do.

He rang the doorbell.

For a long time, there was silence. He rang it again.

Stamping inside turned into, "What the hell? It's dark outside."

Ben opened the door.

"Ms. Sharp. Really? There's nothing for you to do here."

"Rainey's in danger."

Ben started to close the door. Harry did what he'd seen in a dozen family movies and put his foot in the doorway to stop it.

"Oh my…! My foot! You're crushing my foot!"

"Then what did you put it in the door for?"

"I need to talk to you. I have to talk to Rainey."

"You've done enough. Please leave."

Harry took a step back. Ben slammed the door shut.

"Who's that?" Zach said from somewhere in the hall.

"Crazy lawyer lady. Go back to sleep."

"Hungry…"

Harry left the front door, stalked around the house, and stepped back into the shed.

"Plan B."

5:33 a.m.

Plan B involved a ladder. Harry had got it years earlier because someone had offered to clear the gutters for £200 in twenty minutes. Harry declared it was too much for such a job. The man said it wasn't so much the job. It was the equipment needed to do the job. Take the ladder for instance.

Harry was a businessman and didn't appreciate price gouging in any shape or form. He'd said no to the man and his van, gone to the hardware store, and purchased his own ladder. It cost him £398, and he took three days to clean the gutters. At the time, Harry had been a little embarrassed at how stubborn he'd been. Gutter clearing was clearly not his forte. But now, leaning that ladder against the wall next to Rainey's bedroom window, he felt like a genius.

He tapped on the glass. "Rains?" He whispered and tapped again.

A lamp went on inside, then a giggle. "Dusky? Is that you?"

"No, it's not Dusky." Harry rubbed his face. Maybe it was the height, maybe the lack of sleep, or maybe it was because he hadn't eaten in hours. The ladder seemed to sway under his weight. "It's, Da... It's Harr... It's Harriet Sharp."

Rainey pulled her curtains open and stared. She opened her mouth to shout. Harry reached through the window and gripped her hand. "Please. Just listen. It's about Dusk. Please. One minute. I just need one minute."

Rainey pulled her arm free and stepped back. "You're the maddest lawyer I've ever met. Is Dusk okay?"

"I don't have time to be soft about this, Rains. I'm going to tell you something you won't want to believe, but please, please listen to me. Dusk is after your money, and he'll do anything to get it."

Rainey reached for the window and started to close it.

"Wait!" Harry gripped the frame with both hands. "I was just there."

"Where?"

"Dusk's house. I saw him, his brother, and two thugs he hired. They were talking about their plans. He's going to take you out tonight."

"I know. He sent me a text. We're going for dinner. Just us. He said I need some spoiling." Rainey smiled. "I agreed."

"He's going to…" Harry hesitated. He said the word *kill* in his head, but it sounded too hard. *Murder? No. Bludgeon? Assault?* "He's going to hurt you, Rainey. The car that almost hit you? That was Grayson Hamilton."

"What makes you say that?"

"I heard them."

"Them who?"

"Grayson and Dusk. I heard them talking."

"When?"

"Just a few hours ago. I was at their house."

"You were at their house at two in the morning?"

"Three."

"You're speaking crazy."

Harry kept talking. "He's going to get you hospitalised and use that to get your brothers out the house, and the men he hired are going to rob the place. Now, I don't give a flying duck about the stuff."

"What did you just say?"

"Dusk is going to hurt you."

"No, after that."

Harry frowned. "He hired men to rob the house."

"Before that."

"What? Nothing. That's it."

"You said *flying duck*."

Harry shrugged. "I…okay. Well. That's not really the point. The point is you're in danger. Rainey. Please. You can't go out with him tonight. Give me time to come up with another plan."

Rainey frowned. "You've already done too much. If my brothers find you here, they'll probably get a restraining order. They'll definitely call the police. I'm fine. Dusk has no intention of hurting me. That other lawyer is going to reinstate the will anyway. The whole three-day rush is off. I'm fine. Everything's fine. Go home, Harriet. Please."

Rainey went to close the window.

"Wait." Harry reached through the window and picked up a pen and Post-it note from Rainey's desk just below the windowsill. He wrote down the number of the phone Betuine gave him. "Call me. Any time. For anything. Just call me if something goes wrong or if you can't reach your brothers. Anything. Will you, please?"

Rainey took the paper and stuck it on her mirror. "Fine. Now please go." Gently, like she didn't want to cause offence by closing the window too fast, she locked Harry out. Then, she waved and smiled before she drew the curtains.

Harry pressed his head against the windowpane. Inside, there was a knock on Rainey's bedroom door.

"I'm sleeping. Go away," she mumbled.

"You okay?" Ben asked.

"Course I am."

"Okay." After a brief pause, Ben said "okay" once more.

Harry knew that Ben would be standing at Rainey's door for a while longer. Just to be sure she was alright. Just to be sure she was safe. Just in case she needed anything. Just like Harry had done a thousand-thousand times in his life.

"Get more sleep. See you in a bit." Ben gave the door one last tap.

"Hmmmmm." Rainey rolled over and would be asleep in a moment.

Harry climbed down the ladder.

It was 6:02 a.m.

9:46 a.m.

After sitting in the shed for more than three hours without a single worthwhile idea entering his head, Harry made his way back to the Two Beagles Inn. Conscious that his clothes were worn, dusty, and wrinkled, his shoes were dirty, his hair was a mess, and he had sweated through his shirt a dozen plus one times, he decided breakfast and a shower would clear his head and help him think.

Dusk was taking Rainey out for dinner. He had all day to think of something. Anything.

Harry ignored the other guests, filled a plate from the breakfast buffet, and took it upstairs. He closed and locked the door behind him and sat on the bed.

Not hungry anymore and not caring how unkempt he looked and felt, he turned his face away from the mirror and let the tears flow.

Sleep. That's what he needed. Sleep, then food, then a shower.

Harry lay his head on the pillow and sat up when he noticed a single piece of paper that looked like it had been torn from a spiral bound notebook.

It had no words, just a drawing. It was perfect in its detail. Elegant in its simplicity. A butterfly. Wings outstretched. Even though it was just a line drawing on a page, Harry got the sense that the insect was in flight.

The drawing didn't feel like something Jonesy put on his guests' pillows instead of the standard foil-wrapped chocolate. Was it some message from Betuine? What's the story about how a flap of a butterfly wings changes everything? Was it a warning? Had Jack Harker left it?

Harry stared at the drawing, and in a moment, it went from a beautiful piece of art to a warning, or a threat, or a cruel game from some evil devil stalker. Had Dusk Hamilton put it here? Was it a threat against Rainey?

Harry put the piece of paper back on the pillow and paced the room.

12:56 p.m.

Having held out for as long as he could, Harry showered, cleaned up as much as possible, ate everything he'd piled onto the plate that morning, and made use of Max Tiggis' Bentley to drive back to his family home.

This time, he didn't park two houses down. This time, he drove all the way to the front door.

Harry didn't bother to knock. He doubted the boys would open the door. Instead, he walked around the back. It was a family habit; the kitchen door into the backyard was always unlocked, and unless it was blowing a gale or snowing, it was almost always wide open.

"Fresh air," the children's mother, Harry's beautiful Jess, had always said. "A house has to have a flow of fresh air."

Like the fresh air, Harry walked in uninvited.

Zach, his mouth full of food as usual, stood up. "Ben! It's the crazy lady again. Ben!"

With a book in one hand and his phone in the other, Ben stepped into the kitchen. "You have to be kidding me. What the hell do you want?"

Harry pulled two of the kitchen chairs out and pointed to them both. "I want you to shut up, sit down, and for once in your lives, listen. Rainey's in trouble." When the brothers didn't sit, Harry kept talking. "I went to Hamilton's house last night. He's got a plan to hurt your sister. Tonight. He's going to take her to dinner, then he's going to fake a mugging to get you out the house. And I don't think he cares if she lives through it or not."

Ben sighed. "Ms. Sharp. I can see you're distressed. I don't know what's going on in your life, but this is getting out of hand."

"Are you honestly saying you trust Dusk Hamilton with Rainey?"

"No," Ben said. "I bloody despise the man, but that doesn't mean he's going to hurt Rainey. Why would he?"

"As a distraction. For money. He's trying to get you all out of the house so he and his friends can rob the place. He's already tried twice."

Ben put the book and the phone down. "What are you talking about?"

"The close shave with the car? That was Hamilton's brother. The food poisoning? I imagine that was them too."

"How do you know about that? And anyway, why would he kill Rainey? He'd be the first one the police looked at. He's not that stupid. They're engaged, not married. He gets nothing no matter what."

"Of course he's not stupid, which is why he won't be the one doing the stealing. He's hired a couple of guys from out of town. He'll be with you and the police playing the fiancé role."

"What are you all talking about?" Rainey walked into the kitchen, pulled out a chair, and sat.

"Nothing, Rains." Ben put an arm around Harry's shoulder and ushered him out the kitchen door. "Ms. Sharp is having another bad day and is just leaving."

Harry turned to Zach. "You've seen how aggressive he is, Zach. What if he turns that on your sister?"

Zach touched his bruised face. "He wouldn't dare."

"Really?" Harry looked between Zach and Ben. "Tell me, hand on heart, you don't think Dusk Hamilton won't dare. Tell me that, and I'll go right now, and you'll never see me again."

Rainey stood up. "Dusk won't do anything to me. Ever. He loves me. Oh, my God. You're driving me crazy. Dusk and I are getting married and there's nothing you can do about it. Nothing!"

Rainey threw her mug into the sink, shattering it against the stainless steel.

For a moment, Zach, Ben, and Harry stared after her. Then, Zach said, "If there's a way to get rid of him, I'm up for it."

That was all Harry heard thanks to Ben shoving him into the back garden and closing and locking the kitchen door.

Harry stood at the back door for a moment then made his way to the shed, sat on the same bench facing the window that gave him a complete view of the back of the house, and he waited.

7:03 p.m.

Headlights sent beams around the side of the house at exactly 7:03 p.m. Shouts came from inside the house. The only words Harry heard clearly were Rainey's: "Don't you dare follow me!"

A car door slammed, and tyres crunched gravel. Five minutes later, Zach and Ben jogged out the back door, got into the car Harry used to own, and drove away.

"Good lads." For the first time since Harry arrived back in Fairfig, he felt a smile spread over his face.

7:09 p.m.

▼

Betuine Harker paced the halls of her domain. Corridors upon corridors. Doors upon doors. Each one leading to some kind of therapy or treatment, education, class, apprenticeship, or spa session.

Usually, when she walked the halls, it was to revel in the thing she'd created.

"This used to be nothing more than an empty room, you know. Bare stone floor. I added the linoleum, then the walls, then the chairs. All these therapy and treatment rooms were my idea. Therapy itself was my invention. Mine!"

Whoever she was with would smile politely and know they were in it for the long haul. Betuine would hide a little grin. Not only had she planted the idea for linoleum in the human psyche, but she'd also planted the joy of telling and retelling the story in the aged mind and an inability to escape the telling and retelling in the mind of the youth.

Betuine opened a door on a basket weaving class. Twelve, burley men licked bleeding fingers as they entered their fourth decade of learning how to weave baskets from river reeds.

"Not so easy, is it?" A red-haired instructor shredded a basket like a female weaver bird showing disdain for yet another nest that didn't meet her standards. "What do you say when someone makes or does something that makes your life easy? Like weaving baskets, or making dinner, or sweeping the floor, or washing your manky underpants. What do you say? Say it!"

"Thank you."

"I can't hear you!"

The men all shouted "Thank you!" in unison and kept on weaving.

The instructor turned to Betuine. "Hello, Mayor Boss-Lady. Would you like to address the students?"

The men paused and held their collective breaths. Betuine shook her head. The men sighed and kept weaving.

Betuine studied them for a moment then stepped out, closed the door, and rummaged through her dungaree pockets for her phone. She dialled. Harry Blunt picked up.

"Have you got what I want, Harry?"

Blunt paused, then he said. "I do. Hang on. He gave me a card."

"He gave you a card? You met him?"

Silence on the line. "He lives on a farm in the middle of Cumbria. I'll text you the address right now. I'll have to hang up to do it."

Harry Blunt hung up. Thirty seconds later, Betuine stared at an address to something called *DMC Farm* then at a photo of a business card. *Jack Harker, Attorney* was embossed across the middle.

Betuine opened the door to the basket weaving class again. She looked at the men. They were all doing time for being unappreciative husbands, weak partners, and bad fathers.

"Put their fingers in salt," Betuine said.

The men gasped.

"You heard the mayor. Salty dip. Salty dip."

The men dipped their chapped, cut, bleeding fingers into bowls of salt ground just fine enough to wriggle deep into the tiny cuts. Every one of them winced.

"What do you say?" Betuine commanded.

"Thank you," the men said in unison.

The instructor smiled. "They'll make better husbands, partners, and fathers next time round, Betuine. I'll see to it. They'll all learn their lesson."

Betuine nodded. "See that you do."

THE INCIDENT

Harry put his phone into his pocket and took a breath. That should get Betuine Harker off his back. He got into the Bentley.

The kids were sorting things out themselves. He wasn't interfering. Rainey was with Dusk. That was certainly a risk, but her brothers knew all about it and had followed them. Now he had to do what he couldn't do when he was alive. He had to sit, and wait, and do nothing while they sorted things out.

"I can do that. A nice supper, a shower, and a nap. Because that's what parents do when grown-up children are living their lives."

Harry took a breath, held it, and drove away from his family home. When his lungs started to ache, he hummed a tune he used to hum to Rainey during thunderstorms. There weren't any words to it, just a tune. He imagined that if there were words, they'd include a wild story about unicorns and guinea pigs. That's the kind of thing Rainey liked as a child and still did.

Harry paused at a traffic light. Drizzle dotted the windscreen, turning the view outside into a spotted mosaic of reds, greens, blues, and all the hues in between. He opened the window and let the cool, damp air in.

There was a time when he used to worry about wet roads and inexperienced or aging drivers. He used to switch his windscreen wipers onto high speed and be on alert for every car on the road.

Now, he let the rain fall. He watched the drops form kaleidoscope colours until someone touched their horn behind him. Harry reached an arm out the window and waved. The driver behind him would think he was apologising. Harry was really just saying hello.

I should have said hello more often, he thought as he accelerated from stationary to snail's pace across the intersection, causing the person behind him to hoot a little more. Harry smiled and said hello again.

"Fish and chips," he said. "That's what I'll have for supper."

He had just parked outside the fish shop three blocks from the inn when his phone rang.

"Harriet! Ms. Sharp. It's Rainey."

Harry took a breath. Soft rain, fish supper for dinner, a call from his baby girl, and extra days in Life. The world couldn't get better. Then, Harry sat up straight.

"What? What's wrong? Are you alright? Where are your brothers?"

"I don't know. Something's happened. Dusk and I…"

"What? Oh, my God! Where are you?"

"I'm at the park. By the stairs. Next to the bridge by the river."

"What happened? Are you alright?"

"I'm fine! I went to get coffees. I left Dusk talking on his phone. I came back, and he's at the bottom of the stairs."

"Hurt? D…" Harry dropped his voice to a whisper. "Is he dead?"

"No! Oh, my God, no! I've called an ambulance. He's not… He's not dead."

"Have you called your brothers?"

"They'll explode! I haven't."

"I'm coming to you now." Harry heard sirens in the distance. "I think that's the ambulance on the way. Don't move. Don't do anything. I'm on my way."

Harry took every shortcut he knew through Fairfig and arrived at the biggest park the town had to offer just as the ambulance did.

Rainey was sitting next to Dusk Hamilton, holding his hand. The boy was unconscious but breathing, albeit erratically. The medics moved her aside and did their job.

Rainey stood a few feet away from them and watched. Terror and worry dripped down her cheeks. Harry couldn't help it. He couldn't stop himself. He reached out, pulled her in, and hugged Rainey tight.

For a moment, he felt her body go rigid like she wasn't sure she should be hugging this strange lawyer person who had managed to destroy and make her day all at once. Then, she relaxed, wrapped her arms around the body Harry was wearing, and held tight.

"Thank you for coming," she whispered.

"I wouldn't be anywhere else."

The medics lifted Dusk Hamilton onto a gurney and wheeled him to the ambulance.

Rainey pulled away from Harry and ran to them. "Can I come with?" she asked.

The medic helped her into the back of the ambulance and shut the door. Harry ran to his car and followed, dialling Ben's number as he went.

Ben answered. "What is it, Ms. Sharp? What do you want?"

"Get to the hospital now. You and your brother. There's been an accident. Where are you? Where's Zach?"

"I don't know. Is it Rainey? Is Rainey alright? What happened?"

"Rainey's fine. It's Hamilton."

There was a pause. "When you say accident, what exactly do you mean?"

"He's not dead if that's what you're asking. Rainey needs you. Get Zach and go."

Harry hung up, put the windscreen wipers on high speed to clear the drizzle off the window, and looked around him. No sign of Grim "Call me Grimmer" Reaper. There was that at least.

The butterfly drawing on his bed. Had Grim left that, warning him about the ripple effect? Had he caused this?

"The idiot probably just slipped on a step. Some random mugging."

Some random mugging.

That's what Hamilton had said would happen to Rainey. Maybe the random mugging went wrong and they got Hamilton instead of Rainey.

Harry punched the steering wheel. There he was about to order fish and chips for dinner while his daughter was in mortal danger. Mortal danger!

Harry rubbed his face and slapped himself on the cheek. "Idiot! Getting all loving Life! Have you forgotten why you're here?"

He glanced at his reflection in the mirror. Betuine Harker's body looked back.

Harry accelerated to get through an amber light and got to the Fairfig hospital just as Dusk Hamilton was being wheeled in through the double doors.

Harry didn't follow them in. He looked instead for Rainey. She was wrapped in Ben's arms, then in Zach's. Then, all three hugged like they used to do when they were kids: arms around each other, heads together, whispering so no one else could hear.

That was the one part of their childhood Harry was never a part of. They always broke up their huddle before he got close. It was a sibling thing, and it filled his heart with so much joy to see it that he had to wipe tears from his face.

Ben pulled away first. "Ms. Sharp."

"Please call me Harriet."

"Harriet. Thank you for getting to Rainey so soon."

Harry nodded. "Is she okay?"

Ben glanced back. "She'll be fine. Any news on the Hamilton family?"

Harry shook his head. "I haven't contacted them yet. I'm sure the hospital will."

Zach groaned. Rainey dropped her head.

"Must we?" Ben asked. "Rains? Do you have their numbers?"

Rainey shook her head. "Only Dusk's."

Harry nodded. "Leave it with me."

Leaving his children huddled back together under the bright lights of the hospital entrance, Harry went inside wishing and hoping, more than anything he'd ever wished and hoped before, that Dusk Hamilton would simply die.

FAMILY GATHERING

It took one phone call from the nurse's station to the Hamilton family residence for Mum and Dad Hamilton, their remaining children, and a whole lot of noise to arrive.

Harry was only familiar with Grayson, the younger boy. Harry studied the family. He could see the resemblance. Father to sons. Mother to daughters. Only one child had the round features her mother brought to the gene pool, but that stopped short of the eyes. Like the rest of them, their eyes were hard and cold, darting around the ward until they settled on Harriet Sharp.

"Who are you, and where's Dusky?"

Without introducing himself, Harry pointed towards the hospital room where Dusk Hamilton lay infused with tubes, drips, and machines doing their utmost to prolong the life of another stupid human.

AI can't take over fast enough, Harry thought. *It would see right through Dusk Hamilton and cut his oxygen off.*

The Hamilton family glanced into the room, then Mum Hamilton took charge. "Grayson, find the canteen and the vending machines. You two," she pointed toward the daughters, "find the toilets. Dad, you and I will find the docs. Hop to it."

With the Hamilton family on their appointed missions, Harry glanced around him. Busy people all running and rushing. No one watching. He could do it. He could just squeeze a little critical pipe.

Before Harry could make his move, Rainey and the boys walked into the ward, still hugging each other close. Harry did a quick calculation in his head. There was time. It wouldn't take much. He could put an end to Dusk Hamilton himself.

"So, you gonna tell me what happened?"

Harry started and turned. Coffee cup in hand, Grayson Hamilton sauntered into the ward. He searched it like he'd find the cause of his brother's demise under the bed. Then, he pointed at Ben and Zach who'd followed him into the room. "You did this. This was all you."

Harry tapped Ben and Zach on the arm. "Leave before it gets messy. They're emotional. Look after Rainey. Go home. I'll stay here and keep an eye on things."

Ben searched the ward for Rainey and finally found her huddled on a plastic chair beside the nurse's station.

"Rainey won't go," Ben said.

"Rainey must go. Get her out of here. Where were you two? You left her alone with him tonight. After everything I told you, I thought you were following her."

Harry held Ben's glare. The young man finally turned and walked away. His face was set hard. He leaned close to his sister, whispered, and pulled her to her feet.

With Ben, Zach, and Rainey safely away, Harry watched Grayson Hamilton lean over his brother.

Harry almost took a step forward, but the rush of the Hamilton family to the boy's bedside stopped him. Having established the location of the various amenities and conveniences, they flipped the switch on drama.

"What did he say?" Dad Hamilton pressed forward first.

"Oh, my boy. My beautiful boy. Oh, my Lord, save him." Mum Hamilton pressed her hands to her face and let herself be led to a chair by her oldest daughter.

The other two siblings hung back like they were ready to take dibs on Dusk's belongings.

Grayson leaned close to Dusk.

Dusk's hand fluttered in the air then sank to the bed.

Grayson glanced up, fixed a stare on Harry, then went back to listening to his brother.

Dusk's hand lifted one more time and pointed. The Hamilton family all stared at Harry.

Harry took a step back, bumped into someone, turned, and stared at the balding, polished head of Grim "Call me Grimmer" Reaper.

"Well, this is a surprise." Grim took a breath and let it out slowly. It made Harry think of all the times he'd walked into Zach doing something stupid in the name of art.

"This has nothing to do with me, or Rainey, or any of my kids."

"That's not exactly what I'm referring to." Grim pulled his notebook out of his top pocket. "I came here to collect a certain Miss Rainey Blunt. But unless she drops of a perfectly healthy heart attack, it seems she's not going anywhere."

Harry's belly clenched, sending a hum and a buzz into his chest and making him catch a breath in his throat. "She's not?"

Grim tapped the notebook with the fingertip. "The complication, if you can call it that, is that Dusk Hamilton wasn't on my list, Harry." Grim held his notebook up for Harry to see. "You see?"

Harry looked at the page. Name upon name was listed in neat calligraphy. Last on the list was Rainey Blunt. No Dusk Hamilton.

"Now," Grim pulled a short pencil out of his pocket, "I like order, Harry. I like things to go as planned. My dear sister, on the other hand, she likes chaos. She's finding this whole situation very funny. I, however, have to deal with the consequences of all this change. I have to pick up, transport, and deliver an unscheduled soul. I have to explain, to Judge Sweet no less, why he's on the bus. And do you know what I'm going to say, Harry?"

Harry shook his head.

"I'm going to say it was you," Grimmer looked down on Harry, "considering you're not supposed to be here, Harry Blunt. Considering you're supposed to be in Port Harker preparing yourself for an 87-year sentence for basically doing exactly what you're doing now, i.e., interfering." Grimmer cleared his throat and took another breath. "Well. I suppose that's not really my concern because you're going to be the one to do all that explaining."

Harry glanced back at Dusk Hamilton. Machines beeped and screeched alerts. Medical staff pushed the family back and applied all their medical know-how to resuscitate him.

"You can't take me back." Harry patted the body he was in. "This is Betuine Harker's body. She let me come here. We made a deal."

"I don't think that deal stands anymore." Grim licked the end of the pencil, pressed it against the white page, and started to write. "You broke the rules."

"I did no such thing. I didn't do this."

Grim ignored Harry and turned his attention to his notebook. He used the eraser at the top of his pencil to rub out *Rainey Blunt.* He blew the bits of worn eraser off the page, causing them to spark and the fluorescent lights in the ward to dim for just a second. Then, he wrote two new words: *Dusk Hamilton.*

The moment Grim put a dot after the boy's name, two doctors and three nurses took a step back. One of the doctors shook her head and glanced at the clock on the wall. Mum and Dad Hamilton wailed. The two sisters shrugged. Grayson Hamilton grinned.

▼

Dusk Hamilton's body lay still and quiet. To the human eye, nothing moved. The room took on the stillness that only comes with death.

To Harry, who had seen the other side and now could not unsee it, Dusk Hamilton's soul tore out of his body and lunged.

Harry stepped behind Grim, who sighed and shook his head. Dusk's soul vibrated and expanded, then contracted into a tight ball, and finally took on a form that was more like him in Life. His body rattled like it just noticed it was empty and could finally relax. The soul screamed a silent scream and reached out for Harry.

Harry pressed himself against the hospital wall as Grim pulled a black sack out of his pocket and threw it over Dusk's head.

"I'll not have bad behaviour on my watch," Grim snapped.

Dusk's soul paused, turned in a small circle, and stood still.

"More like it." Grim licked the tip of his pencil once more and turned his attention back to his notebook. "As for you, Harry Blunt."

The only thing that stopped Grim writing Harry's name in his book was a ringing phone in Harry's pocket.

"That's Betuine," Harry said. "Should I take it?"

Grim scowled. "Hand it over." Grim answered the phone. He nodded. He shook his head. He started to say something then stopped. "As you wish," he finally said. Then, he hung up and handed the phone back to Harry.

"Seems Betuine's deal still stands. She said she'll be in touch."

Grim took Dusk Hamilton by the arm and led him down the hall past doctors and nurses, patients and visitors, none of whom so much as looked their way. Harry watched them disappear around the corner. He heard the bus door hiss open and Dusk Hamilton shout, "Harry Blunt! You bastard! I'm going to destroy…" There was a scuffle then silence.

"You had one chance," Grim muttered. "I said no trouble. Do you want to travel all the way with the hood? Do you?"

"Blun…"

Silence.

Harry took a breath and turned when someone tapped his shoulder.

The doctor who'd declared Dusk Hamilton officially dead frowned. "Are you alright?"

Harry glanced over the doctor's shoulder at the still, deceased form of Dusk Hamilton. He pressed his lips together and put on a mournful face. "I'm fine. I'm alright. Thank you." He patted the doctor's arm and left the ward. Only when he stepped into the lift did he lift his skirt an inch above his knees and do a little dance.

▼

Karma leaned close to the monitors that filled a wall in the hospital's security office. *Filled a wall* was an exaggeration. It was more like three screens, one of which had *Match of the Day* on replay.

The security guards had been overcome with an overwhelming urge to get real coffee from a deli three blocks away, giving Karma a chance to watch Harry Blunt up close.

"That's my guy." She grinned as Harry threw his arms in the air and danced a jig in the elevator, stopping just in time to straighten his skirt and his face and leave the hospital with all the dignity of those who mourn the newly deceased.

She flicked through the security cameras in the hospital until she came to Ben, Zach, and Rainey all huddled at the front door. The moment 'Harriet Sharp' stepped out of the hospital, the three split apart like they'd been caught stealing cookies.

Karma kept smiling and flipped through the security cameras. She only stopped when she came to Grayson Hamilton. He was standing around the side of the hospital building, lighting a cigarette, watching the Blunt trio. He inhaled the smoke then let it out slowly. He did that until the Blunt family left the hospital grounds, then he dropped the cigarette stub on the ground. He didn't stamp it out or even look to see whether it had landed on dry grass, paper, or anything else that might catch fire and burn the whole place down.

"I'll remember that," Karma said, and she left the security office just as the security guards came back, full on coffee and cake.

DAY 3:

IT WASN'T AN ACCIDENT

With the kids all back home and settled and the morning sun starting to rise, Harry sat in the park and took a breath.

Dusk Hamilton was dead. Rainey was safe. He smiled. Rainey was safe. With no one but Bernie the beagle out for a sniff and a few birds to witness, Harry threw his arms in the air and laughed.

He had one day left, and his baby girl was alive. The person who was going to kill her was dead, gone, and in Port Harker.

"Have I done it?" Harry said to the tree he leaned against. "Have I done what I came here to do? I did, didn't I? I saved Rainey's life. She'll keep on living. Grim took her name out of his book. I saw it with my own eyes. I saw it, Bernie." He scratched the dog behind the ears. "She'll have time to find her way. I've changed…" Harry paused and looked around him, then he whispered to the dog. "Did I actually change the course of my baby's destiny?"

Harry smiled, leaned back, tilted his face to the sky, and let the sun soak into his skin. When his phone rang, he let it ring for a while before he picked it up.

"Hello?"

"Ms. Sharp! Oh, my God. Please come to the house. I don't believe this is happening."

"What?" Harry sat up. "Rainey? What's happening?"

"The police are here."

"For what?"

"Before Dusk died, he told his brother that it was Zach who pushed him down the stairs. The police are taking him in for questioning. We need a lawyer, Harriet. They're leaving now. Right now. You have to come. I'm following…" There was a rustling on the line. "I want to come with!"

"It's okay, Rainey." Ben's voice came across loud but calm. "Just stay here. Tell Ms. Sharp to meet us at the station."

"Ben!" Harry heard Zach shout, equally loud but definitely not calm. "What the hell? What's going on here? Get your hands off me."

"Zach. Settle. They're doing their job. Don't fight. Just…Zach. Oh for heaven's sake. Look…"

There was a crash. A door slammed. Rainey sobbed. A voice Harry didn't recognise said, "We're not interested in a fight, sir. Get him out of here."

"Rainey!" Harry was up and running. "I'm coming! Get to the police station. I'm on my way."

Harry arrived at the Fairfig police station to find cars parked out front, a few officers ambling around, birds singing in the trees, and no one - no one - seeming to appreciate how quickly his day had gone from *bliss* to *are-you-kidding-what-just-happened?*!

Harry parked Max Tiggis' Bently in a slot reserved for *staff only*, slammed the door shut, and marched up to a police officer dressed in a uniform so overloaded with the tools of her trade that Harry wondered how she could possibly find a way to sit comfortably or move freely. "I'm looking for Zach Blunt and Ben Blunt. Zach was brought in for questioning."

The officer shook her head. The tightly wound bun pulled her face back, making her look a little more serious than perhaps she intended. "Speak to the officer at the front desk. Inside."

Harry noticed the young woman glance down from Harry's grey mop of a head to his dusty shoes.

Two days in the same suit in a borrowed body. He checked the buttons on his jacket were done, polished the shoes on the back of his legs, rubbed his face, and ran his fingers through the knotted grey mass that had seemed to grow an inch since he'd arrived.

"Thank you," he muttered and strode up the stairs.

Another officer stood behind the glass-fronted reception area. "Help you?"

Harry glanced around the institutionalised entrance of the station. It was like they were giving visitors one warning: this is the best it gets; careful what you say here. One wrong step and you end up in a room just like this but without the pretty posters.

The posters displayed warnings for every type of criminal tendency, from drugs to child abuse, discrimination to pickpocketing. Helplines for everyone, from children to the suicidal to the aged, encouraged people to call and talk. There were even posters detailing how to spot loneliness in your neighbour as though being lonely was as criminal as carjacking.

"I'm… ahhh…" Harry glanced around him and gripped the front desk to keep himself steady. "I'm here to see Zach Blunt. His brother, Ben Blunt, should be here too. And their sister, Rainey Blunt."

The officer nodded. "And you are?"

"Their father…" Harry said before he could stop himself.

The man glanced up. "Excuse me?"

Harry shook his head. "Their father passed away. I'm their lawyer. Harriet Sharp. Their family lawyer."

The officer nodded. "Take a seat. I'll call through."

Harry nodded but didn't move from where he stood. The officer frowned, then shrugged, and ambled into an open-plan office. He filled his mug with coffee before he picked up the phone and talked to someone, glancing only briefly at Harry, then turning his back as though the rest of the conversation was none of Harry's business anyway.

"Ms. Sharp?"

Harry turned. "Yes. Harriet. Harriet Sharp. Lawyer." Harry noticed his eyes wouldn't stop blinking, so he squeezed them shut for a moment. "Hay fever," he said.

The police officer in front of him wore a loose, navy suit with a crumpled white shirt and flat, black lace-up shoes. Her hair was tied back in a loose ponytail. She had no makeup and looked like she needed a good night's sleep and maybe a holiday.

Harry unbuttoned then rebuttoned his jacket, gave up on his appearance, and tried to smile.

The officer held out a hand to shake. "Tough for us girls to stay tidy in a crazy world, right? DCI Wallace. You the lawyer?"

Harry nodded and took out the ID that came with the handbag and body.

"How long have you known the family?"

Harry shrugged. "Years. Their whole lives. Ahhhh… In one way. Just a few days in another. As their lawyer, I mean. Right. This isn't… Can I see him?"

DCI Wallace studied Harry for a moment, then let a small smile touch her face, only to vanish a moment later. "Of course. Come on through."

Harry followed the woman down a hall that looked like it could have been any office. He passed open-plan desks with computers, screens, piles of papers, the occasional wilted pot plant, and half-filled coffee cups. And much like any other office, a few people ambled about, not even pretending to look busy.

Harry almost had to jog to keep up with DCI Wallace. "Can you tell me why Zach was arrested?"

"No one has been arrested, Ms. Sharp. We're just asking them a few questions. Why don't you have a chat with them first? I'll get the coffees in."

"Them? I thought it was just Zach."

"Or would you prefer tea?" The detective stopped at a door with *Interview Room 3* etched into a plaque at eye level.

Harry nodded. "Tea. Sure. Four sugars. For them too? Where's Rainey? Their sister. Where is she?"

"She's with a family liaison officer down the hall. She's alright."

The detective opened the door and let Harry in.

Ben Blunt stood then sat down again like his legs weren't able to take his weight.

"Ms. Sharp, thank you for coming."

Harry sat down opposite his son, reached out, and took his hand. Ben pulled away.

Harry took a breath. "From the beginning," he said. "What happened?"

Ben rubbed his face. "I'm not really sure. We all got home after the hospital. Rainey was in a state, as you can imagine. She went upstairs. Zach went to his studio to break things. He does that when he's stressed. I was in the kitchen because that's what I do when I'm stressed. The doorbell goes, and it's the police. That's it. They started asking questions about last night. Where Zach was. Where I was. Our relationship with Hamilton. Then, they say they have a few more questions and they wanted to bring Zach in for questioning. So, we all came. And here I am. Is Rainey okay? Is she alright?"

"She's down the hall. What are the police saying happened?"

Ben shook his head.

"Ben?"

"I don't know, alright. I don't know. They won't let me talk to Zach."

"Where was Zach last night?"

Ben rubbed his face. "We were both out."

"Out where?"

"I was at Two Beagles. Mostly. Zach was…I'm sorry."

Harry folded his hands in front of him and waited. The more you pushed Ben, the slower he got. Harry waited until the man took a breath.

Ben kept talking, "You tried to warn us. I should have listened. Rainey saw us following and got upset, so we backed off. I need to talk to Zach," Ben whispered, then cleared his throat. "Ms. Sharp. I think they're saying one or both of us killed Dusk Hamilton. I tried to call…" Ben looked guilty like he'd almost confessed to cheating.

"Did you call Jack Harker?"

Ben nodded. "I left a message. He hasn't called back. I know you're a family lawyer, and we haven't been the best family to deal with. You can't know how much it means to me that you came here as fast as you did. But is this your expertise? Can you help?"

Harry stared at the chipped fingernails on his hands. "Let me make a phone call. Just sit tight, okay? Don't say anything until I'm back. Just wait."

Harry stood just as the door opened, and DCI Wallace ambled in with a cup of tea.

"I need to see Zach Blunt," Harry said.

"If you like." Wallace put the tea on the table. "He's just confessed to shoving Dusk Hamilton down the stairs with the intention of, to use his words, 'seeing his skull smashed open and his puny brains turned to fish food.'" Wallace turned to Ben. "You can go."

Ben stood. "Are you insane? He didn't do that. He couldn't have."

"Why, Ben? Why not?"

"Because…"

Harry squeezed Ben's arm. "I said don't say a word until I get back. And you, DCI Wallace, can keep your tea. You leave these kids alone until I'm back and they have proper representation. Stop trying to manipulate them."

Ben picked up his jacket and started to follow Harry out. "They said I could leave."

DCI Wallace nodded. "Sure. We're just having a conversation. And since your brother's confessed, I guess there's nothing more to talk about."

"He didn't do anything."

"What makes you so sure of that?"

"Because I… I mean…" Ben sat back down and dropped his head in his hands. "Harriet?"

Harry pointed at the policeman. "You leave my kids alone until I'm back."

DCI Wallace sat in the seat across the table from Ben. "You and your lawyer close?"

Ben glanced up. "I guess. I don't know…" He shook his head. "I have nothing to say at this point."

Harry nodded. "Good lad."

The only private space Harry could find to make a call was a storeroom packed from floor to ceiling with toilet rolls and cleaning fluid. He wondered for a moment whether Betuine had a hand in stocking police station supplies. Seems like something she'd enjoy. He searched his pockets, and then the very useful handbag, for the card Jack Harker had given him.

"I don't believe I'm doing this." Harry closed his eyes for a moment and pressed the card to his chest. "Please answer," he whispered, then he dialled Jack Harker's number.

Harry was prepared to argue, persuade, beg, and plead with the man to step in and help. What he wasn't prepared for was, "I'm already here."

The line muffled like Jack Harker pressed it against his chest. "I'm here to see DCI Wallace. Jack Harker. The Blunt family lawyer."

More muffles. Harry stepped out of the storeroom into the hallway and peered through the glass windows in the doors just in time to see DCI Wallace shake Jack Harker's hand.

"Jack Harker," Harry heard through the open line. "Good to meet you. Yes, Ms. Sharp is a colleague. She deals with family estates. I handle things when families go wrong."

DCI Wallace said something Harry couldn't hear. It made Jack Harker laugh. "Don't you know it," he said and hung up the phone.

A door opened down the hall, and Jack Harker, dressed in a hand-stitched tailored suit and a sunset red tie with a proud blue goose on it, ambled down the corridor like he'd been to the Fairfig police station a thousand times.

▼

Betuine Harker was tidying stationery. It's what she did when she was stressed. "Rows. Neat rows," she muttered. "Everything in its place. Everything has a place. There must be order. Then, you can predict things. When things are tidy, you can find them. When things are tidy, you know where things are. They stay where they belong. They don't wander off and get lost."

Betuine grabbed a box of No. 2 pencils and threw them on the floor.

200 perfectly sharp, exquisitely crafted, red and black striped pencils scattered and rolled under the racks.

"I won't have this! I won't be toyed with!"

She pulled her phone out of her pocket. She dialled Harry Blunt's number.

"Blunt!" Betuine shouted into the phone.

"What? Yes! What do you want?"

"I want you to do what you said you'd do."

There was a pause on the line. "I did. I got you your father's address. I gave it to you."

"You said you'd do whatever it took to save your Rainey."

"I did. Dusk Hamilton is dead. She's safe."

"So it would seem. Killing Dusk wasn't really in the plan, was it Harry?"

"I didn't kill him."

"Your interference led to a series of events of which that was a consequence. You broke the rules. Your actions led to an alteration of another's timeline. That means the deal has changed. I want my father here. In Port Harker. Face to face. With me."

"Your father isn't interested in returning to Port Harker, Betuine."

"He doesn't have to be interested, Harry. He just needs to be dead. Make it happen."

"You're asking me to… How do you… What?"

THE NEW DEAL

Before Harry could say another word, Betuine Harker hung up.

Harry stared at Jack. Jack smiled. "Everything alright, Ms. Sharp?"

Harry shook his head and held up his phone. "Just…fine." He put the phone in his bag. "I'm fine, Mr. Harker. Thank you for coming."

"Always happy to help out family."

Harry forced a thin smile on his face in response to the frown from DCI Wallace.

Jack Harker drummed his fingers against his phone and turned to the detective. "Before we talk to our clients, can my colleague and I have a moment please?"

Huddled in a tiny canteen with a coffee machine that promised an array of flavoured coffees but clearly didn't deliver based on the layer of dust and absence of cups, Harry took a breath.

"Did you get Ben's message? Is that why you're here?"

Jack glanced around the room and smiled like he was in a place that comforted him. "Unfinished business, Harry. I still don't know what my daughter's up to. I don't mind that she's looking for me. I do mind when lives are influenced as a result. That's not right in the universal scheme of things. My rule, you see..." Jack Harker opened the cabinet doors in the small canteen. It was empty except for one pack of coffee filters. "My rule is to blend in with the world, Harry, not make waves. So, I'm here because I've been keeping an eye on things. I saw you all heading this way, and figured I might be able to help. And yes, I got Ben's message."

"Betuine wants to talk to you. In person. In Port Harker. As in face-to-face."

Jack Harker dusted off the coffee machine and pressed a button. Nothing happened.

"And you said?"

"I said nothing! She hung up."

Jack pulled the machine away from the wall, wiped the plug down, and put it into the socket. Nothing happened.

Harry rubbed his face. "She's changed the deal. Can she do that?"

"Did you break the rules?"

"I don't know. Maybe. I guess Dusk Hamilton wasn't quite ready to die."

"Did you kill him?"

"No! Bloody hell. Of course I didn't. And neither did any of my kids. It was an accident. A random mugging."

"The mugging that should have seen Rainey dead, buried, and in the TV room?"

"Details," Harry said, and he slumped against the wall.

Jack Harker pulled the back off the machine, tugged the wires out, twisted two of them together, tucked them in again, put the back of the machine on, and pressed the on button. Lights flashed and blinked. He opened the narrow cupboard below the coffee machine. A stack of paper cups stood alone on the bottom shelf. He took out two. "Seems you have a choice, Harry."

"Exactly what choice do I have?" Harry wiped sweat from his face.

"I can either stay here and help your children, or you can send me back to Port Harker so I can help my child. And just so you know, I won't make it easy. You'll have to look me in the eye and put a knife in this body's heart. What's it to be, Harry?"

"I thought you were immortal. How's stabbing you going to work?"

"This body isn't immortal. If I break it, I have to get a new one. Unlike you, I can do that. I return to Port Harker, get a copy of the same body, and come right on back here."

"Unlike me?"

"When you die, you get a whole new life, Harry. A clean slate. I get to go on with all my memories and identity uninterrupted."

"Do you want to go to Port Harker?" Harry groaned, "Not that I'm saying I'm okay about stabbing you. I can't believe I'm having this conversation."

Jack shook his head while he balanced a cup on a small tray and pressed a button that said Hazelnut Cappuccino. The machine coughed and whirred, pulled fresh water from the mains, and gurgled out a frothy beverage. "If I did, I'd have made my own way there long ago." He handed Harry the cup and filled the second cup with the same. He took a sip. "Delicious."

Harry sipped and disagreed.

Jack pulled out one of the only two chairs in the room and sat. "I've been on Earth for over 1,500 years, Harry. I arrived around the time humans discovered coffee, which, I have to say, has only been good for around 100 years and interesting for around 10. So, forgive me for loving my double-caff, hazelnut, oat milk, semi-froth, extra hot, macchiato with cinnamon on the top." Jack smiled and sipped. "So, what's it going to be?"

"Betuine's struggling in Port Harker. She said you gave her the job and just left her."

Jack nodded. "I did."

"How could you do that? She's your child. How could you leave her knowing she was struggling."

"She asked me to."

Harry blinked. "She did?"

Jack leaned back. "I'd been running Port Harker for 40,000 years before Betuine got interested in the family business."

"Family business? What about…"

"Angels, demons, heaven, Lucifer, fallen angels, hell, and all the rest? Do you really want to know, Harry?"

Harry didn't move. "If I do?"

Jack Harker took another sip. "The apple tree story isn't about good and evil, Harry. It's about the choice between knowing or not knowing."

"Ignorance is bliss," Harry whispered.

"Isn't it?"

"Not really. Did you really run all of the afterlife?"

"No. I just did a job I was given by the powers that be."

"Who are the powers that be?"

"Not my story to tell, Harry. Betuine." Jack Harker paused. "Betuine's heart is bigger than mine will ever be. I can't say I ran anything. I just kept an eye on souls as they rotated through lives not getting any better or smarter. Betuine had ideas. She had this whole plan. Port Harker exists because she built it, and now she wants out. But that's not how things work, right? You can't just quit because life and death get tricky."

Harry took one breath, then another and held it. "I don't know what to do."

"You get to choose. Who would you like me to help? Your kids or mine?"

Harry looked up at Jack Harker and studied the man. His eyes had a glimpse of Grim in them. They were hard and soft at the same time. "Betuine really asked to be left to run Port Harker?"

Jack nodded. "She said she could do a better job than me. She said she would modernise. And she did. That gave her new problems. It's her job to work things out."

"It's your job to help her."

"Is it though?"

Harry blinked. "Of course. You're her parent."

"Is she a child?"

"It doesn't matter how old she is. She's still *your* child."

Jack smiled. "You ever study a butterfly coming out of a cocoon, Harry? It's a battle. Hard struggle. The thing is, if someone were to cut that cocoon so the butterfly can get out more easily and more quickly, you know what would happen?"

Harry stared at Jack Harker and finally shook his head when he realised the man wasn't going to carry on until he got an answer.

"The someone who cut the cocoon would feel all hero-like," Jack Harker continued, "but that beautiful creature would not be able to fly. So, I ask again. What do you want me to do, Harry? I can't do both. I either stay here and help you and yours, or I go back to Port Harker."

Squeaking footsteps down the hall stopped Harry speaking. DCI Wallace put her head around the corner. "Hey, who fixed the machine?" She pulled a cup out and pressed a button for Coffee Black. "You two ready? Your clients are getting nervous."

Jack studied Harry. Harry studied the floor. Finally, he said in a whisper, "My children need your help."

Jack Harker drained his paper cup and threw it in the bin. "DCI Wallace, lead the way. Let's see if we can't sort this out before dinner. You eat dinner I take it?"

DCI Wallace laughed. "Just not with you."

"You'll not be disappointed. I make the most incredible pancakes."

"Pancakes for dinner?"

"Breakfast."

DCI Wallace laughed again. "That's completely inappropriate and I should be offended. I'll pass but thanks…"

Their voices faded as they strode down the hallway to Interview Room 3, leaving Harry alone with a cooling cup of powdered coffee.

"Ms. Sharp?"

Harry looked up to see Rainey, pale and tear-streaked. "Oh, my Lord, Rainey." Harry hugged his baby girl, and she hugged Harriet Sharp back.

"What's happening?" Rainey finally pulled away.

"Jack Harker is with your brothers."

Rainey wrapped her arms around her slim shoulders and folded herself into the plastic chair furthest from the door.

The phone in Harry's pocket rang. He stared at the screen and picked up.

"Harry?" Betuine's voice was soft and slow.

"Betuine."

"My old man isn't here yet. What are you doing?"

"I'm working on it. I haven't seen him yet. You have to give me time."

"You don't have time. You have less than half a day left. Are you conning me, Harry? Are you actually trying to trick Me? Capital Me? Queen B?"

Harry swallowed and turned around so Rainey couldn't see his face. "You're asking me to do something impossible."

"Really, Harry?"

For a moment, there was silence on the line, then finally, Betuine spoke. "Judge Sweet told me this would happen. I didn't want to believe her, but she's always right. That's why she's the judge, I guess. She doesn't believe you'll achieve anything at all. You've interfered with Rainey's life, Harry. Again. All that led to Dusk Hamilton dying before his time. So, do you know what the Judge has done? Do you want to know?"

Harry swallowed and glanced back at Rainey. He cleared his throat. "What?"

"She gave Dusky a suspended sentence. Do you know what that means?"

Despite the warmth in the air, the skin on Harry's arms prickled. Betuine didn't pause. She kept talking.

"It means he doesn't choose his next life. I do. I get to say where and when he goes next. And I've thought long and hard about it, Harry. I mean, this is people's lives. You don't take any of this lightly. Right, Harry?"

Harry rubbed his hands over his face. "What are you going to do, Betuine?"

"I'm going to hold onto Dusk Hamilton until Rainey conceives her first child."

Harry squeezed his eyes shut. Betuine whispered into the phone. "Dusk Hamilton is going to be Rainey's firstborn, Harry. Get the job done. Send my father to Port Harker or your grandchild will be Dusk Hamilton. And he will come back to Life with all his fury, all his hate, and all his sociopathic joys. If you think Rainey's in trouble now, Harry Blunt, you wait to see how a child like Dusk Hamilton will tear her apart."

"You can't do this."

"I can, Harry. A deal's a deal."

Harry kept the phone next to his ear long after Betuine hung up.

"Ms. Sharp?" Rainey said. "Is everything alright?"

Harry turned to Rainey. He smiled. "Sure. Of course. Everything's… Everything's fine, Rainey. Maybe we should get you home. Mr. Harker will take care of things here. Just give me one moment."

Harry crossed the hall, stepped into the first restroom he came to, leaned over the toilet, and threw up.

"You alright, ahhhh… Ma'am?" A young constable pulled up his zip and stepped away from the urinal.

"Fine!" Harry snapped. "Can't you see how goddamn fine I am?"

▼

Sitting on a park bench across the street from the Fairfig police station, Karma flipped through her notebook. The bench creaked when Grim sat down beside her.

"Brother." Karma reached out her hand and took his in hers.

"Sister." Grim squeezed her hand in return.

"My pages for Rainey Blunt are blank. I can't see where she goes next."

Grim nodded. "She's not in my book either. Unheard of."

Karma leaned her head against the tree behind her and watched the leaves dance in the breeze. "I was going to get lunch at the little diner in the square. You want to join me?"

Grim smiled. "In light of the current goings on, I think that's a fine idea. Feels like we haven't talked in a while."

Karma and Grim looped arms and ambled down the road and into Fairfig Square, looking like any normal, impossibly exotic, unexpectedly beautiful tourists.

"You have money on you?" Grim asked.

Karma bumped into an old man who'd just berated a teenager for riding her bike on the pavement. "I do now." She grinned and held up his wallet.

TROUBLE ALL ROUND

Harry was standing outside the station breathing deeply when the taxi pulled up. Grayson Hamilton got out, scowled at Harry, and ambled up the stairs and into the building. Harry followed.

"Is Rainey Blunt still here? I'm here to give her a ride home."

The duty officer picked up the phone beside him and made a call.

"Why are you taking Rainey home?" Harry asked from the door.

Grayson Hamilton turned around and looked at Harry like the desk he was leaning against was a bar, Harry was a beggar, and the view outside extended to the dock against which his yacht was moored. Grayson looked Harry up and down and saw a dowdy, crumpled woman with puffy cheeks and red-rimmed eyes. "You're the lawyer."

It wasn't a question, so Harry didn't answer.

Grayson put on a concerned expression as seamlessly as he did the white shirt on his back. "It's not good for her to be alone at a time like this."

"You accused her brother of assault and murder. You told the police Zach did this."

Grayson shrugged. "Somebody has to take the fall."

Harry blinked. "You saying you know he didn't do it?"

The boy shook his head. "That's not what I'm saying at all. My brother was a shit. Everyone knows it. We're all just doing the sad thing because that's the thing to do."

"It was considered an accident until you told the police otherwise."

Grayson shrugged. "Maybe it was. Maybe it wasn't."

"What in God's name are you saying?"

The man smiled and turned to Rainey as she stepped into the reception area. "There she is. I'm here to take you home."

"Home? I don't…I'd rather stay here."

"Can't stay here, Miss," the officer behind the door said, "unless you're waiting for someone."

"My brothers."

The officer shook his head. "Wouldn't wait for them today if I were you. Get some rest. Let your friend take you home."

"He's not my friend."

Grayson gasped and, for a moment, looked as hurt as any human can look under the circumstances. "Rainey. It's all I am. Please let me take you home. We've got a lot to talk about." Grayson pulled Rainey close to him and pressed his lips to her ear. Rainey paled, then nodded and smiled. Grayson kept talking. "Our only concern is to see you right. To look after you. Where else are you going to go? To that empty house that isn't even really yours anymore?"

Rainey covered her face with both hands for a moment like a child playing peek-a-boo. Then, she crossed her arms over her chest, glanced at the police officer, and then looked at Harry. "Alright. I suppose," she whispered.

Harry blocked the door. "I don't think you should leave. I'll come home with you. To your house."

Grayson Hamilton reached around Harry and opened the door. "Rainey was Dusk's fiancé. As good as family in our book. I promised Dusk I'd take care of her. I always keep my promises. Don't I, Rains?"

Rainey blinked, nodded, and walked out of the station. Grayson Hamilton glanced back at Harry, grinned, then put his arm around Rainey's waist.

"What the hell is going on?" Harry murmured as the taxi pulled out and drove away.

He got into Max Tiggis' car and made to follow them only to be blocked by another car. A serious-looking woman scowled from behind the wheel. "That's my space," she announced.

"Congratulations," Harry snapped. "If you let me out you can actually take it."

By the time Harry got out of the police parking lot, the taxi carrying Grayson Hamilton and Rainey was gone.

"Right," Harry muttered, and he headed for home.

▼

By the time he got there, there was no sign of the taxi. The house was quiet. The house was locked. Harry looked in through every window downstairs and tested all the doors. The kitchen door was unlocked and standing open. He went inside. He'd lived in that house his whole life, so he knew what it felt like empty. And at that moment, the house was more empty than it had ever been.

Computers, TVs, paintings, and small antique pieces that could easily be lifted and carried were gone. The bigger pieces had been left behind. Everything else of value had been taken. The two men clearly worked out that the numbers were better now that the boss was dead. Harry didn't care.

"Rainey?" he called. Just being thorough. "Rainey?"

Harry walked slowly through the kitchen, touching the surfaces with his fingertips. Like the memories were embedded in the granite, they surfaced unbidden. The first time Zach tried to make pancakes. He made such a mess. They were cleaning flour out of corners and crevices for a month. Ben made them the next Sunday, and they were perfect because he'd read a dozen recipes and had been practising all week. This infuriated Zach, who ate them in protest.

Harry smiled and breathed the air in. A combination of lavender, wood varnish, baked bread, and polish wove a tapestry of memories through his senses. The clean, warm smell of home.

Every corner, wall, and stair had a story. The coat rack where the coats lived, only changing in size as each child grew. The key holder. That was Zach's first real art project. He came home with a dozen saw cuts on his hands and his prize: an owl-shaped key holder, varnished to a shine, with six hooks for claws.

The painting in the hall, all framed and protected from the elements, was Zach's second real piece of work. Oils in the style of Van Gogh. He spent the whole of dinner giving alternate explanations for why the great artist took his ear off.

Trophies on the bookshelf in the hall were all Ben's. The prize winner.

Harry studied the art on the walls, the family history on the shelves, the certificates, and the congratulations. All Zach and Ben. Rainey hadn't created, produced, or achieved anything that warranted anything more than a high school certificate.

"Rainey?" Harry called again. Silence.

He picked up his phone and dialled her number.

She answered. "Ms. Sharp? Harriet?" Her voice was tight and high.

"Rainey, where are you? I'm at the house."

"I'm at the Hamilton house. Please, help me. Help me. I'm in trouble." She sobbed.

"Don't move," Harry said. "Better yet, get out and wait for me on the pavement out front."

"I can't," Rainey whispered, and her line went dead.

"Oh, no you don't." Harry ran through the house and drove to the Hamilton private residence so fast that he attracted the attention of the local constabulary.

▼

"Excuse me, Ma'am?" A young officer and his partner got out of the police car behind Max Tiggis' Bently, which was parked with three wheels on the pavement outside the Hamilton household. "We'd like a word."

Harry glanced back. "I'm seeing my client. I'm a lawyer. If you want a word, you'll need to get in line."

"I don't think…" The officer turned to his partner like he wasn't quite sure what to say next. She nodded encouragement. "Things don't work that way."

Harry scoffed. "Young man, you have no idea how things work." He turned his back on the officers and strode up the path.

By the time he reached the front porch, the two officers had caught up.

Grayson Hamilton opened the door. His eyes went wide for a moment then smiled. "Ms. Sharp. The lawyer. And the police."

Harry walked in. "Rainey?"

The Hamilton family had gathered in the living room. Smiles turned to scowls. They didn't try to hide the lit BBQ or disguise the smells of sauce and sausages wafting in through open patio doors. Ice clinked in jugs of iced margaritas and Dusk Hamilton's sisters didn't so much as glance up from their cake slicing duties.

Rainey was standing in the middle of the room, her arms folded tight around her chest, the Hamilton clan touching and hugging her, telling her everything would be alright and that they knew it wasn't her fault. They'd sort everything out. This was her home now.

She sobbed when she saw her lawyer.

Harry was an arm's reach away from Rainey when Grayson stepped between them.

"Everything's fine." Grayson put his arm around Rainey. "Isn't it, Rains?"

Rainey stared at Harry and nodded. "Yes. Fine." She swallowed. "I just want to talk to Ms. Sharp about my brothers."

Grayson smiled. "I'll come with you."

Harry held out his hand. Seems Grayson wasn't expecting much force from a middle-aged woman. He stumbled back. "I'll take it from here, Mr. Hamilton. Thank you. Rainey, let's find a quiet place to talk."

The two police officers stood at the door. Grayson glanced at them, held up his hands, and stepped back.

"Why are the police here?" Rainey whispered. Her hands shook as she gripped Harry's arm, and they walked down a hall littered with fake Persian rugs and monochrome photos of half-naked people.

"I was speeding. I think they want to take me to task, but I don't have time. Their presence is useful though, don't you think?"

Rainey shook her head, and tears fell down her cheeks.

"Talk to me, Rains. What's going on?"

"Grayson's blackmailing me."

"How? What's he saying?"

"He says I have to give him money. A lot. Every month. Or marry him."

"You don't have to do any such thing. That's ludicrous. Why is he even trying?"

Harry stopped when Rainey touched his arm. "He saw me push Dusk down the stairs," she whispered.

Harry stopped. "Excuse me? What?"

Rainey ducked into a bathroom and pressed herself against the wall behind the door. Harry followed her in, closed and locked the door, and double checked to make sure no one could get in.

"We went for dinner. He got distracted by some friends. I saw his phone. I saw what he said about me. I saw the plans he had for the house. He used such ugly language. We fought. Harriet, he got so angry." Rainey sat on the toilet seat. "We started to walk home. He went through the park. I followed him. He said so many horrible things, and I just…" She swallowed and looked up at Harry, those wide eyes pleading for help. "It wasn't an accident. I want to say it was, but I don't know. What you said about him wanting me for my money. I saw it in his eyes."

"It was an accident. It was self-defence. Why didn't you say anything?"

"Ben said he was going to sort everything."

"Ben knows what happened?"

"No. He just said he was going to sort everything. Then, Zach confessed. Then, things got complicated. Then, Mr. Harker arrived. Then, no one would talk to me. They just kept telling me to go home. Then, Grayson arrived."

"What exactly did Grayson say to you?"

"At the police station, when he whispered to me, he told me he saw me push Dusk, and if I don't do what he wants, he'll tell the police everything. He'll say Ben and Zach were there too. He said he has photos of me. I don't know what to do."

Harry sat on the edge of the bath and ignored the ringing phone in his pocket. He could handle anything except Betuine Harker.

"Okay," he muttered. "Right. We've got this."

The phone kept ringing.

Rainey sniffed. "I'm so sorry," she whispered.

Harry squeezed her arm. "It's okay. We'll work this out."

The phone rang again. Harry picked up. "What? What do you want?"

Betuine Harker chuckled. "You know what I want, Harry. Time is running out. Get it done. I've got Dusk Hamilton right here in my sweaty palm. One slip and he lands back in Rainey's life. Tick, tock, tick, tock." Betuine hung up.

Harry switched the phone off and looked at Rainey. He saw the tiny baby he held in his arms the day she was born. The toddler he carried in a basket on his bike because she'd fallen off her own and didn't want to try again. The young girl who didn't know how to swim because she didn't like getting wet. The teenager who got everything she wanted and everything done for her because she said she couldn't do it on her own. The young woman who had no idea what to do with her life, who had no purpose, and who had no future. Harry closed his eyes and rubbed his chest until it hurt. "I'm so sorry, Rainey. I'm so sorry, my sweet."

Rainey stared at Harry, seeing only the lawyer she felt was her last and only resort.

"How are you feeling right now, Rains?"

Rainey sobbed. "What do you mean?"

"Take a moment to feel everything. How do you feel?"

"Scared. I feel scared. I feel alone."

"Like you have no control?"

Rainey nodded.

Harry held her hand. "I feel the same, Rainey. There's only one way out for both of us. This is going to be hard. You're not going to like it. I'm not going to like it, but we're going to do this together."

"I don't understand."

Harry stood up and pulled Rainey to her feet. Harry straightened the plaid skirt, tucked in the shirt, and buttoned the jacket. He wiped the tears from Rainey's face.

"When someone has something you want more than anything in the world, Rainey, they have power over you. When you have secrets and desires that others are privy to, they have control over you. Do you understand?"

Rainey shook her head.

Harry pulled out the phone and dialled.

"Who you calling?" Rainey whispered.

"Someone who's blackmailing me."

Betuine picked up the phone. "Better be good news, Harry."

"I won't do it, Betuine. Rainey is tough enough and strong enough for anything you and Hamilton have to throw at her. She's smart. She's tougher than she knows right now. She's got a heart of solid gold and courage like steel. There's nothing you can do that'll break her. So, you do your worst. She can handle it."

Before Betuine could say anything, Harry hung up and put the phone back into the handbag.

Rainey stared at Harry. "I don't understand."

Harry smiled. "Someone was blackmailing me too, thinking that if they threatened you, they'd get me to do something terrible. They're banking on you not being strong enough to stand up for your Life. For your brothers. For what's right. It's time for you to step into your power and wield it, Rainey. How you live your Life is up to you. It's all yours. It's your choice."

Harry hugged Rainey then left the bathroom, walked down the hall, and entered the living room. The two police officers were still at the door.

"Ms. Sharp." They both had their notebooks out. "You can't just walk away from us like this. We're the police."

Harry nodded. "Quite right. So you are."

Harry didn't pause, didn't hesitate. He kept walking to the door, past the officers, and down the path. The police glanced at each other and followed.

Harry had just reached the garden gate when Rainey called from the door. "Wait, Ms. Sharp. Officers, please wait."

Harry turned. The police turned.

Rainey shrugged off Grayson Hamilton's grip. "I killed Dusk Hamilton. It was me, not my brothers. They're covering for me, or each other, or...I have no idea what they're doing." She turned to Grayson. "You gross little pig," she said. "You won't get anything. You certainly won't get me."

With her head held high, Rainey Blunt strode down the path and up to the officers. "I killed Dusk Hamilton. I want to say it was self-defence. I think he planned on killing me first, but I pushed him down the stairs with every intent of getting rid of him." She walked through the garden gate and squeezed Harry's arm. "Will you meet me at the station?"

Harry nodded and grinned at his daughter as she stood at the police car waiting to be let into the back seat.

The two officers stood still for a moment. The senior of the two shook her head. "Every day a surprise." She glanced at Harry. "I'm still giving you a ticket."

"Happy to pay it," Harry said. "I'll follow you in."

Harry watched Rainey climb into the police car, shoulders back, head held high. Her eyes were clear and bright, like she was seeing the world from a whole new view and liked what she saw.

The Hamilton family watched Rainey being driven away.

Harry smiled, got into the Bently, revved the engine enough to spin the wheels in the grass, then followed the police from a law-abiding distance.

His phone rang. He pulled it out his pocket and threw it out the window.

▼

Karma and Grim watched the cars drive by: the police officers, quiet and stoic; Rainey, calm and serene; Harry Blunt, grinning like an idiot.

"Didn't see that coming," Grim said.

Karma smiled. "Kinda love it though, right? Betuine's going to be fuming right now. Is Rainey in your book yet?"

Grim flipped through the pages. "No. Her end in this life isn't decided yet."

"What does that mean?"

"Means she's got control of her destiny."

"If she knew that, do you think it would help her make different choices?"

"Not sure." Grim put his notebook away. "Humans don't necessarily make better choices just because they know what's at stake."

Karma leaned against the tree and watched the Hamilton house. She took out her notebook and filled in a few lines. A crash came from inside. Then, a scream.

"What are you doing?" Grim studied his sister.

"Cause and effect, brother. I'm not doing anything at all."

Grim and Karma ambled down the road as the Hamilton family ran out of the house with smoke and flames billowing out the backyard and setting fire to the living room.

"Hungry?" Grim said.

"Always. Steak. Rare. And fries. Then cake. Stupid people put me in the mood for cake."

THE ART OF STEPPING UP

"She's covering for us," were the first words Harry heard as he stepped into Interview Room 3 at the Fairfig police station. Jack Harker leaned back in his chair and watched the siblings.

"Welcome to crazy." He smiled and pulled a chair out for Harry.

DCI Wallace studied the three from the corner of the room and said nothing.

"I am not covering for anyone." Rainey pulled her hands into two fists, planted them on the table, and half stood only to sit when Constable Speeding Ticket stepped forward. "I did it. He had some plan to rob our house. He had a plan to get rid of me. We took a shortcut through the park. We came to the top of the stairs. I knew what he was going to do, so I did it first. I pushed him, and I meant to kill him."

Ben turned to DCI Wallace. "You can't believe this. She's just covering for us. You can see she's not capable of doing this. She's just a girl."

Rainey stood up so fast her chair flew across the room and hit the wall behind her. "How dare you? Ben Blunt. How dare you? I can't say it's your fault. Heavens knows I've used this little-lost-helpless-girl thing to get you to do pretty much anything I want, but I'm tired of being perceived as weak. I'm tired of playing helpless and useless. I'm tired of everyone taking over for me. I'm tired of not living my life like I should and want to. I'm tired of you fixing things. I'm extremely tired of being told what you think I am or am not capable of! I'm a grown-up, adult woman fully capable of killing another human being. So capable, in fact, that I did it!"

Zach and Ben stared at their sister.

Officer Speeding Ticket picked the chair up and moved it out of Rainey's clearly deranged reach.

Jack Harker did his utmost to keep a straight face but finally let a smile escape.

Harry grinned. "That's my girl," he said.

DCI Wallace shook her head. "Okay. From the beginning."

Telling her brothers to shut it and grabbing the chair from the constable, Rainey sat down and glanced at the tape machine on the table between them and the video camera ahead of her. "Are we going to record this? I don't want to have to repeat myself more than necessary."

DCI Wallace took her seat and pressed record. "Interview with Rainey Blunt, Zach Blunt, and Ben Blunt. Also present are lawyers Harriet Sharp and Jack Harker. Myself, DCI Wallace, leading the interview with Constable Jones in attendance. Rainey." DCI Wallace said. "Have you been read your rights?"

"Yes, I have," Rainey said.

"Do you understand them?"

"Yes, I do," Rainey said.

"Alright. From the beginning."

And Rainey started to tell her story from the beginning.

For the first time in their lives, Ben and Zach didn't interrupt their sister or try to take over or correct her. For the first time in his life, Harry listened to his daughter.

"That's what happened," Rainey finally said. "I realised that if I didn't stand up and tell the truth, then my brothers would pay for something I did, and being blackmailed by Grayson Hamilton of all people means

I'd be paying a horrible price for the lie for the rest of my life." She glanced at Harry. "When you tell the truth and take responsibility, you take your power back. Isn't that how it goes, Ms. Sharp?"

Harry smiled. "Yes, love. That's how it goes."

For a moment, there was silence. No one moved until DCI Wallace cleared her throat. "Ben Blunt, Zach Blunt, do you have anything to add, confirm, deny, or retract?"

"I don't…" Ben started.

Rainey held up her hand. "Enough, Ben." She turned to her brother with a steel in her eyes that Harry had never seen before. "Stop it. Stop protecting me."

Ben gripped his sister's hand and kissed it. "I take back my confessions. I'm sorry for messing everything up."

"You wasted police time is what you did." DCI Wallace tapped her fingernails on the table. "Zach Blunt?"

Zach let out a sob, reached over to his sister, and hugged her. "I'm sorry, sis. I'm so fricken sorry."

Rainey hugged him back. "You have nothing to be sorry about. I'm the murderer in the family."

"Oh, my Lord." Ben threw his arms in the air. "You don't make the first thing you take real responsibility for killing someone. Damnit, Rainey! You start with broken windows or something. Can't she be given some kind of…"

"Ben!" Rainey stood up. "You're as bad as Dad." Harry gasped. Rainey kept talking. "He protected me from everything too. Every time I did something wrong or couldn't work something out, he said it was someone else who'd messed up, or the weather wasn't right, or the water was too wet, or anything except me needing to step up."

Harry pressed his hands into his lap. Out of the corner of his eyes, he saw Jack Harker look his way.

Rainey sat down. "I've got to do this, Ben. I know it's crazy and big, but it's real and it's the right thing to do. Would you rather I lived with a lie? Would you really rather spend time in prison for something you didn't do? This is what's happening. There'll be no negotiation." Rainey turned to Jack Harker. "Mr. Harker. You're a good lawyer. I like you."

Jack smiled. "I like you too, Rainey."

Rainey nodded like the deal had already been done. "I'm not sure of our financial situation right now, but I need representation."

"Your financial security is solid. I'll see to that. Consider me hired."

"DCI Wallace, would you mind if I had a word with Ms. Sharp alone before whatever happens next happens?"

DCI Wallace paused for a moment and nodded. "Sure. She's still the family lawyer, I take it?"

Rainey nodded.

"You have five minutes."

▼

Alone for the first time since the Hamilton's bathroom, Rainey sighed.

"You remind me of my dad," she finally said.

Harry shook his head. "Really? How's that?"

"He was always there when I needed him. Always trying to fix things."

Harry let his head drop. Tired. That's what he felt. Suddenly. Not as tired as he felt the day he first died. But close. Like part of him had already left the world, and the rest of him just needed to catch up but the weight was too much to carry.

"He shouldn't have." Harry looked up at Rainey and saw her smiling through tears that weren't there a moment ago. "He should have let you grow up," he said.

"You tried."

Harry blinked as Rainey reached across the table and touched the smooth, tired face belonging to Harriet Sharp. "I'm either going crazy, or you're extremely weird. Either way, I can't explain it. I don't know how this is possible or if I'm just imagining things."

Harry frowned. "What is it, baby girl?"

"I know it sounds strange, but I can see my dad in you. Am I losing my mind?"

"What makes you…" Harry cleared his throat. "What makes you say that?"

Rainey smiled. "I don't know anyone else on the planet who says *flying duck* quite like my dad. And you said it the day we met."

"Flying duck? Oh. My goodness. You… What? Of course… Well… I knew your dad. I must have heard him…"

Rainey looked up and blinked. "If this wasn't so real, I'd think I was dreaming. There's someone behind you."

Harry glanced down at his hands. The flesh, blood, and bones belonging to Harriet Sharp began to crumble to a fine, white ash, leaving just him, Harry Blunt, back in his dressing gown with no slippers to call his own, behind.

Rainey half stood then sat again. She covered her mouth with her hands to keep her words inside.

Taking a breath, Harry smiled. "It's okay, Rains. You're not going crazy. You're not dreaming."

Rainey pointed to the tall black man behind her father, then she touched the ash on the table where her lawyer's hands had been a moment before. "I don't understand."

"Harry," Grim said. "You have 41 seconds left."

Harry sighed. "You'll find out one day, Rainey, that Grim Reaper doesn't give you much notice." Harry reached out and rested his very own hands on Rainey's.

"You are a tiny part me, a tiny part your mother, and all the rest is you. Your heart, your courage, your soul, and your might. I have to go now."

"30 seconds," Grim added.

"But you've got this."

Rainey smiled through tears. "I've got what?"

"Life, Rains. Your whole life. Messes, chaos, love, fear, hardship, responsibility, dreams. The works. It's all up to you. You have a chance to live it now. On your terms. And you can do anything. You proved that today."

"I killed a man."

Harry nodded his head. "It embarrasses me that I approve. You killed a bad man. Don't make a habit out of it. Just pay the price, and then live. Do everything that scares you."

Rainey wiped her face. "I'm going to learn to swim."

"And ride a bike," Harry said, feeling Grim's hand on his shoulder.

"And drive a car," Rainey said.

"And fall in love," Harry said as Interview Room 3 faded.

▼

The last thing Harry saw before he took Seat #87 on Grim's bus was Rainey being led out of the interview by DCI Wallace with Jack Harker touching his daughter lightly on the back and whispering in her ear.

Harry tried to get comfortable, but the seat was too soft, the back was too hard, and the crying behind him was too loud. Ignoring the "Don't Disturb The Driver" sign, he crowded around Grim as he put the bus in gear and edged forward.

"How angry is the judge?" he asked Grimmer.

"Bad as I've ever seen her, Harry. You need to be ready. Now sit. I refuse to be late."

Harry took a breath. "Okay. I just need a minute. I can do this."

"You don't have a minute, Harry. We're arriving in…" The bus swerved and shuddered to a stop. "Oops. Darn it."

▼

Betuine Harker paced the length of The Great Hall. It was where she came to think and plan. Arches rose above her, joining in a mosaic so grand and glorious that those who saw it called it a portrait of Heaven.

"Bloody idiots," Betuine mumbled. "Like they've ever been there. How'd they know? Harry Blunt will never see it." She bunched her hands into fists and boxed the air. "Never!"

Her shout bounced off the cathedral-style pillars, rose up to the ceiling, and bounced back. The stone floor absorbed the sound and sent it down through the circles of the Headquarters for the Education for Life Lessons. Unfortunate souls taking the moment to wish their sentence was over, and they were in the happy arms of the Mink's Tail Tavern, heard Betuine's voice and took it as their answer. *Never.*

"I'm everywhere," Betuine had said before. "I see everything."

And the people in her care believed her.

Betuine glanced at a grandfather clock that stood as tall as four of her. Grim will have arrived. Harry Blunt will be making his way to court.

Betuine strode up to a wall that looked as permanent as the River Styx itself, pressed her hands against the stone four feet off the ground, and pushed. A door opened to a metal spiral staircase going down. She took the stairs two at a time and opened a small, wooden door at the bottom.

The door opened into her precious stationery room. Knowing exactly where she put everything because everything has its place, Betuine went to the 947th row in Sector 97 and reached behind a box of green biro pens. She pulled out a small, round-bottomed, crystal bottle. Except for the cork and wax that sealed it shut, it looked like one of those antique perfume bottles an old lady might once have had on her dressing room table. Betuine peered inside.

"Hello, Dusk Hamilton," she whispered. "Time to do something useful for once in your miserable existence."

THE ROAD TO HELL

The moment Harry stepped into the courtroom, silence descended, and a path cleared before him as though stealing Moses' staff was one of his many indiscretions.

Judge Cammie Sweet peered down at him from her bench high above the gathered souls. Her orange hair spilled out of a purple turban like so many Florentine fountains.

"Mr. Harry Blunt." She didn't smile. She didn't sigh. She said it as fact. "Would you say you've made quite a mess of things?"

"No, your honour. I wouldn't say that at all."

"Some would disagree."

"Some would be wrong."

"Are you calling Mayor Betuine Harker wrong?"

Harry said nothing for a while. Then he said, "Yes, Your Honour. I am."

The crowd didn't make a sound. Their heads pivoted from Harry to the judge, to a side door of the court through which Betuine Harker, dressed in a gold taffeta ball gown, a diamond tiara on her head, and padded dragon slippers on her feet, marched into the room.

"He made a deal," Betuine said. "He didn't deliver. That's the very definition of making a mess of things!"

The crowd cheered in the way captives do when their captor has a terrible idea for someone other than them.

Judge Cammie Sweet held up her hand. "The deal wasn't sanctioned, Miss Harker."

"The fact that I signed the deal makes it sanctioned. Do you forget who owns everything from this courthouse to Eden and all the way to Armageddon?"

"You're the appointed caretaker, Miss Harker. Not the owner. Your father, who is still co-owner, still lives."

"He wouldn't be if Harry Blunt had delivered on what he agreed."

"And the fact that he didn't, stands in his favour."

For no other reason other than to vent her fury, Betuine Harker grabbed one of the clerks by the shoulders, shook him, then threw him into the crowd. To make sure they didn't annoy Betuine, the crowd let the man fall to the floor.

Betuine took a deep breath in, hummed "Ommmmmmmm" for the count of ten, then straightened her tiara, patted down her gown, folded her hands in front of her like some Southern damsel out of *Gone with the Wind*, and said, "Then what do you suggest, Judge?"

"Harry Blunt will carry out his sentence in your employ."

"My employ? I don't need an employee."

"He can help you catalogue your stationery. You've been meaning to do that since you took this job on."

"No one touches my stationery."

The judge smiled. "And that's why you have so much of it. You can have Harry Blunt on the basis that he works for you for the duration of his sentence, which is," the judge held up her hand to stop Betuine speaking, "572 years."

"1,007 years. Not one more or one less."

"472 years."

"That negotiating tactic won't work on me!"

"372 years."

"Fine! Fine." Betuine held her hands up. "He can work for me. But only for me, and he does everything I say."

"Within his moral code." The judge sipped her cappuccino, scowled, and ordered another one. "Hot, please."

"His moral what?" Betuine practically stuttered.

"His moral code, Miss Harker. You can't force him to do something against his grain, so to speak."

"Can I bribe him and corrupt him?"

"You can try."

"Can I threaten him and torture him?"

The judge picked up Harry's paperwork and handed it to the clerk. "Only if you agree to update him on Rainey's progress once a year."

Harry did everything he could to keep the grin off his face but failed miserably.

Betuine scowled. "Fine."

"Fine," the judge repeated and thumped her gavel. "Next!"

▼

Next for Harry was Charon.

Grim watched him join the line leading to the boat at the Port Harker dock. He watched three people throw up, one person pass out, and Charon put a purple stamp of a two-headed dog on Harry's wrist instead of the blue eel stamp everyone else was getting.

Karma joined her brother. "He's not getting his seven days in Port Harker?"

Grim shook his head. "I expect Betuine paid Charon off. The first door Harry walks through will put him in Betuine's world."

Karma stroked the head of her favourite goose. "You think he's going to make it?"

Grim shrugged. "If you asked me that three days ago, I'd have said no. But today? I don't know, sis. I'm tempted to put my money on Harry."

▼

Sitting in the middle of the front row of Charon's boat, Harry held on tight. The purple stamp on his wrist tingled.

"All aboard!" Charon rocked the boat and laughed when half his customers screamed, two more threw up, and one jumped overboard in plain and simple panic. Charon reached in to pull the woman out, got her half back onboard, then changed his mind and shoved her back in.

"Alright, you idiots. This boat will take you straight to Hell. No detour. No negotiation. If you think you're undeserving, feel free to raise your hand," twelve hands shot up, "and I'll be happy to throw you overboard so you can swim there yourself." Twelve hands shot down. "My job is not to coddle you or hold your hair back if you puke. My job is to transport you. And transport you I will. Hold on tight."

He revved the engine and swung the boat away from the peer and into the middle of the Styx. Harry gripped his seat. A girl, no more than six years old with deep, green eyes and a head of tight, dark curls, reached out and took Harry's hand.

"You're alright." Harry whispered and squeezed the child's hand back.

The boat rolled over the waves created by a giant eel who twisted and roiled in the water a foot ahead of them. The eel's head dipped in and out of the waves, its eyes never leaving Harry's.

Harry stared it down. "You don't scare me."

Hitting every sandbank, tin can, dead fish, and human head he could, Charon steered the boat into a tunnel so tall that Harry couldn't see the ceiling. To the left and right of them, the shores were littered with fires that spiralled from oil drums into flaming tornadoes that disappeared into a thick fog above them.

Around each fire, people tried to warm their hands without burning their flesh to the bone. They turned when Charon's boat came into view, ran into the water, and begged to be allowed onboard.

"Anything! I'll give you anything!" a man on the bank screamed, then he pulled out a hatchet, cut his hand off, and threw it. It landed on the floor at Harry's feet. He kicked it away. The child next to him screamed and fell off the bench into Charon's arms. Charon shoved the kid aside, picked up the hand, and tossed it into the river. The hand sizzled and was devoured by the waves.

Harry smiled and helped the child back onto the bench.

A woman on the shore ran into the water to reach Charon's boat but began to melt as though she was made of wax and the water was acid. The girl started to sob. Harry pulled her close. "It's alright. It's just a show."

Charon stopped the boat. "Excuse me? Do you want to say that again?"

Harry stood. "It's just a show. The folks on this boat all have seven days in Port Harker, then some crazy, basket-weaving sentence. Even if they fell into the water, they'd still make it to shore."

Charon shoved people out the way, clambered over the seats, and made his way to Harry. "Is that what you think?"

Harry held his ground. He didn't so much as blink. "I've just spent three days in Betuine Harker's bodysuit as a woman in Life, Charon, wearing a skirt and an actual bra. There's not a lot you can do to scare me."

Charon took a step back and grinned. "Harry Blunt. Who'da thunk. Look at you, all brave and standup'ish. This the new you?"

Harry shook his head. "No. Same old me. Eyes are open. That's all."

"Well," Charon said, "let's see if we can't make you flinch. See that lantern in the cabin? Get it for me will you, Harry? We're going to need it after the next bend in the river."

Harry rubbed the purple stamp on his wrist. It more than tingled. It had started to ache. He looked at the doorway into the cabin. It looked like any other door on any other boat: a small entrance into a wooden, shack-like structure that carried little more than a few books, a deck chair, a chess board, and enough bottles to stock a Saturday night bar in Soho.

Harry held his hand out to Charon. "Been nice knowing you, Charon. I suspect we'll meet again."

On reflex, it seemed, Charon shook Harry's hand. When he realised what he'd done, he frowned, pulled his hand back, tossed the kid overboard, and turned back to Harry. "Get the hell off my boat."

Half the passengers covered their faces and turned away from the girl splashing and gasping for air. Some leaned out and tried to reach her. One jumped in and tried to save her, but they both vanished into the jaws of the giant eel.

Harry shook his head. "You're a sick puppy, Charon." He stepped through the door, and as far as the passengers were concerned, he simply disappeared.

"Oh, stop your ooohs and ahhhs, you numpty-headed morons. Sit down and shut up." Like the fun had been taken out of the journey, Charon steered the boat in a simple, straight line down the middle of the river. The eel had sunk below the surface, and the people on the beach sipped from cans and waved as the boat went by. Charon finally grinned as he pulled his boat into Port Harker Market. "That bastard's going to be trouble," he murmured, and the people on the boat scuttled off, pretending not to hear.

▼

Harry walked through the door on Charon's boat, but instead of finding himself in the small shack filled with books and bottles, he found himself in Betuine's stationery storeroom where he'd first met her the day he made the deal.

"Betuine?" He called from the doorway. "I'm here." He looked at the racks of stuff so covered with dust and grime it had become unusable. "I'll start cleaning? Is that what you want?"

Still barefoot and in his dressing gown, missing the corduroy suit a little, Harry searched the shelves for rags or anything useful. All he found were pens, envelopes, paper, stamp books going back who knows how long, cupcake wrappings, gift wrap, ribbons in tight balls…

"Betuine?"

"Boo."

Harry turned.

"Hey, Harry." Betuine was back in her onesie. She took Harry's hand and led him to the elevator back to Life. "You want to see Rainey? You can. There's a Harriet suit all freshly pressed and clean. I've even updated the wardrobe. All it'll take is one visit. Go drop in on Rainey and the boys, and then do what you promised to do. I'll make it easy on you." She handed Harry a bottle of fresh squeezed orange juice. "It's daddy's favourite. He'll drink it, and before you know it, he'll be on his way here. Painless and simple as can be." Betuine smiled. "Whatcha say?"

Harry looked around the football field of a storeroom. "I say I've got some dusting to do."

Betuine scowled. "Oh, this isn't where you'll start." She took Harry by the hand and led him to the 12th Circle of Hell.

▼

Karma filled a tankard with hot chocolate, topped it with cream and marshmallows, and added a double shot of brandy. She unfurled her legs and propped her six-inch booted heels up onto the desk in front of her.

"Cookie for you, Miss Karma?"

Karma smiled. "Thank you. How's that cute, new little apprentice of yours?"

A ball-shaped man dressed in a prison guard uniform at least one size too small grinned so wide his cheeks turned ruddy. He took the seat next to Karma and adjusted the controls so the security cameras followed Harry and Betuine through the winding corridors of the 12th Circle.

"She's doing great. Thanks for asking. She's working Charon's boats…"

"She's the one going overboard?"

The man laughed and ignored the ringing phone beside him. "She gets eaten by the eel every day and twice on Sunday. Freaks the newcomers out to no end."

Karma laughed then leaned forward. "Oh, my goodness. Is Betuine taking Harry where I think she's taking him?"

The phone stopped ringing. The answering machine clicked on. "Leave a message," is all it said. Someone did.

The security guard zoomed the cameras in. "Poor sod," he muttered and added a dollop of cream to his own hot chocolate.

▼

Harry watched Betuine stride ahead of him. Every few steps, she did a little dance, glanced back at him, and blew him a kiss. He turned around. The corridor behind him was empty. In every way, it resembled a one-star motel with grubby handprints on the walls and worn carpets littered with stains that could be anything from red wine to blood.

But what got Harry most was the smell. Sweat. Not the type humans leak when they've climbed a mountain or completed an hour of hot yoga. The rancid type. The type that spills out your armpits when you're faced with your living nightmares. Your fears. Your worries. The gut-churning sweat formulated especially for public speaking, extreme heights, midnight basements, and deserted forest cabins. The corridor stank of it.

Betuine chuckled. "The cleanup starts here, Harry." She paused at a door with *Family Planning 101* engraved on a brass plaque. Jumping on the balls of her feet, she swung a door open. Harry forced bile back down his throat as he followed Betuine's finger pointing to a mop and bucket. "Time to get busy."

Harry stepped into a room the size of a big-city conference centre. Tables filled the space in tight rows. Each table had a bucket next to it. In front of each table stood a person. There were men and women in equal measure. Each human bent over the table and did everything in their power to keep the baby in front of them alive. They fed it, changed it, hugged it, rubbed it, sang to it, coddled it, carried out CPR on it, then, when that failed, dumped the tiny body in the bucket and was given another one.

Betuine put her arm around Harry's shoulder. "These silly humans are here because Life after Life, they don't get the whole parenting thing right. It's not really that hard, Harry. You just have to love the little bundles of poop and come second to them. That's the bit they don't seem to get."

Harry watched a man drop to his knees as he lost another child. "How long are they here for?"

"For as long as it takes for them to accept that their needs come second to the child they brought into Life, not first."

Harry took a breath and inhaled the stink of rot and fear. "What do you want me to do?"

"Empty the buckets, Harry."

Harry smiled. "On it, Boss." And he started to hum.

"Shut up!"

Harry started to sing:

When Life is done and the race is run.
Will I, will I, will I, ohhh.
When the goose is...

"I said shut up!"

Harry waltzed between the tables, picked up the buckets, and, one by one, emptied them into an incinerator in the middle of the room.

"So, that's how you're gonna play it. Fine. I'll break you, Harry Blunt, because I own you, and I break everything I own in the end. Everything!"

Harry gagged, then grinned, and emptied another bucket.

"Oh, you can keep this up as long as you like, Harry Blunt. When you can't take it anymore, you let me know. All you have to do is go back to Life, hug your kids, and send my old man down."

Harry dipped his finger in the black, rancid liquid oozing out the bottom of the incinerator and painted a number one on the wall.

"What are you doing?" Betuine screamed above the sobbing humans.

"Counting the days when you have to give me the next update on Rainey. Counting the days!"

▼
▼
▼
▼
▼
▼
▼
▼
▼

Port Harker Book 2:

The Fight for Jevanni Cork

Can Harry stay out of trouble?

What happened to Dusk Hamilton?

Does Jack Harker agree to return to Port Harker?

How far is Betuine willing to go?

The Fight For Jevanni Cork is Book 2 in the Port Harker series.

**To get updates on what's coming next,
go here:**

https://tinakonstant.com/port-harker-updates/

THANK YOU!

Well… Port Harker came into my head around 2014, so as you can imagine, a lot of people have been involved to get it into the world.

- Adrian and Jay for the story time sessions!
- Tracey and Maryanne for being incredible early readers.
- My glorious family for the support and curiosity, and for just being plain beautiful.
- Dorian Haarhoff for all your calm, dedicated, diligent, insights, care, and coaching. Thank you.
- Jack, for listening to me prattle on.
- Stacy for her AMAZING LOVE on BookTok!!
- Michele McLaughlin for connecting me with Stacy

Thank you. If you're all up for another adventure, stick around for Book 2!